D0503052

MARIA,
MARIA

MARIA, MARIA

AND OTHER STORIES

Marytza K. Rubio

LIVERIGHT PUBLISHING CORPORATION
A Division of W. W. Norton & Company
Independent Publishers Since 1923

An earlier version of the story "Brujería for Beginners" was published by Dark Horse Press.

"Tunnels" has been reprinted by permission of *The Normal School*, copyright 2016 by Marytza K. Rubio.

An earlier version of the story "Clap If You Believe" was published by Upper Rubber Boot Books in the anthology titled *Choose Wisely: 35 Women Up To No Good* (2014).

Part of "Maria, Maria" appeared in a different form as "Instructions for Assembling an Origami Crane" in *Grimoire* (2016).

For information about permission to reproduce selections from this book, write to Permissions, Liveright Publishing Corporation, a division of W. W. Norton & Company, Inc., 500 Fifth Avenue, New York, NY 10110

For information about special discounts for bulk purchases, please contact W. W. Norton Special Sales at specialsales@wwnorton.com or 800-233-4830

Manufacturing by Lake Book Manufacturing
Book design by Beth Steidle
Production manager: Beth Steidle

Library of Congress Cataloging-in-Publication Data

Names: Rubio, Marytza K., author.
Title: Maria, Maria : and other stories / Marytza K. Rubio.
Description: First edition. | New York : Liveright Publishing Corporation, [2022]
Identifiers: LCCN 2021057315 | ISBN 9781324090540 (hardcover) |
ISBN 9781324090557 (epub)
Subjects: LCGFT: Short stories.
Classification: LCC PS3618.U3225 M37 2022 |
DDC 813/.6—dc23/eng/20220110
LC record available at https://lccn.loc.gov/2021057315

Liveright Publishing Corporation, 500 Fifth Avenue, New York, N.Y. 10110
www.wwnorton.com

W. W. Norton & Company Ltd., 15 Carlisle Street, London W1D 3BS

1 2 3 4 5 6 7 8 9 0

For my Tiger.

Contents

MARIA, MARIA

BRUJERÍA FOR BEGINNERS

Before we begin, did you all place your rum and dulces de tamarindo in the doorway? Yes, cigarettes are a fine substitute for cigars, as long as you all remembered to add three coins to the offering. We include three coins because three is the number of the gatekeeper, the number of the Trinity, the number that is the basic DNA of our spiritual world. I can't answer that, Leyla. Remember the exhausting and circuitous discussion we had when "good or evil" came up during the first week of class? The true identity of the gatekeeper is revealed in the advanced class.

Today we will work on a group project. No, no. None of that. Uncross those arms and stop sinking into your seats. On your desks, I have given each of you a supply kit with items chosen specifically for you. We may have a visitor from the Quantum Physics 101 class next door; the instructor and I have an agreement. If that happens, you may be asked to share your scissors and a pencil. Do not share your gris-gris or your velas, these items are your fates.

Did everyone bring a ruler? Does everyone have scissors? A piece of paper, X-Acto knife, duct tape, cutting board, bandage? Spool of wire, two-gauge; spool of wire, eight-gauge;

copper coil? Agua de Florida, agua de rosa, a live pigeon, paraffin block, and tweezers? Check your supply kit to see that you have one bag of colored sand, glitter glue, and two embroidery needles. I've also brought in an assortment of oils, hierbas, and plants from my own collection. You may use these items to enhance your petition. Please do not use the ammonia or any of the sealed powders without my assistance. Do not touch the vials of mercury, do not test the sharpness of the knives.

Yes, Denise?

The difference is the smell, that is usually how you can tell them apart.

Yes, you in the back. Lissette, is it?

All petitions require payment, and blood is an offering of the highest value. But you should not presume to know the pigeons' purpose.

I understand.

Well, consider this: Take off your left boot and hold it up for the class to see. Class, do you see the supple chestnut leather that once contained the muscle and mass of a living creature? Without it, your classmate would be barefoot. Without such "brutal slaughter," she'd also be hungry and pale. I can smell the chicken cacciatore she had for lunch on her breath and my one good eye weeps for the cochineals who lost their lives to accentuate her cheekbones.

All petitions require sacrifice. Knowing that, ask yourself, each of you, if you can remain in this class. If not, go next door to the physics class; the instructor and I have an agreement.

Leave the supply kit on the desk, Lissette. Thank you and good luck.

Everyone else, please remove your rings, crosses, and hairpins if you have not done so already. Turn off your electronic gadgets, except you, Annalisa. I know your anklet always stays on.

Come in, sir. You are from the Physics 101 class? Welcome. Take Lissette's seat. Please take her bag of fate, it was meant for you anyway, and let's continue.

We will start with Viviana. Everyone please direct your attention to Viviana and her supply kit. This is a kit for love. As we learned from last week's scrying workshop, several of you share this aim to varying degrees and will have similar items. Javier, can you see from there? Pull in closer so you have a better view. Viviana wants to attract love, a new love, a first love.

Yes, sir, you have a question? That is a generous offer. As the only macho in this class I suspect you will be tempted to exert your charm on all my students. But the purpose of this demonstration is education, not fulfilling your carnal desires.

Viviana's kit includes a hummingbird feather, which I won't pass around. Viviana, please hold up your piece of wing. The hummingbird is a fierce warrior, an essential ally for someone who is as shy as our Viviana. I tele-chatted with Viviana last night, and was so pleased she allowed me to make an example of her kit for today's lesson.

No, not telephone, Leyla. Tele-chat.

I'll be brief, since we must submit our petitions before sunset. After crashing our cars in the parking lot of El Super years ago, Viviana and I retained a psychic bond that germinated from our shared susto. I damaged my lower back and she offered the name of her acupuncturist, who helped me tremendously. Viviana was unharmed—her youth and health are a great armor—but I wanted to reciprocate. I began visiting Viviana's dreams to coax her into this class so she could develop new friendships and confidence. And now look at her, hair pulled back and a pretty pink lipstick. Soon she will graduate to a pouty red.

Viviana's pink hummingbird candles should be burned consecutively; she'll light the next one as soon as the previous one is down to its final layer of wax. This ensures a seamless burning petition. After they have burned out, we will inventory Viviana's suitors and chart the burn pattern of the glass. From there, we will determine if we should follow up with an offering of honey and perfume.

Sir. That is an unfortunate attempt at humor. Rohypnol is not an acceptable offering for any divine or human being. Raise your hand the next time you wish to speak.

For those who are ready for a more progressed stage of romantic development, a red Chuparosa, a red Ven a Mi, or even a plain red candle yields impressive results. When you write your names on the candle's glass, make sure your name is always on top of theirs. Always. Full birth names preferred. Do not assume the name they tell you is true, especially in this town. Candle work is futile without the correct address.

You have the most experience with illicit botany, Annalisa, but I wouldn't recommend it to anyone else. You're married, yes? Then I suppose toloache would be feasible to administer daily in liquid form, provided the dose is exact. Jimson weed, class, jimson weed. Distilled and dropped into a coffee cup—yes, or vodka—can make men docile and bring them to a perpetual amorous state.

I asked you to raise your hand rather than interrupt, but yes. You are correct. It is absolutely fatal.

Class, we will learn about the datura species and other potent plants after we return from spring break, but for now you can inspect an example of toloache there on my desk. It is the bell-shaped flower next to the vials of mercury. Toloache is a relative of belladonna, the plant Victorian women used to distill and drop into their eyes to make them dilated and seductive. Don't use belladonna in your eyes. The drops will make you blind and dead.

No, Denise, I do not recommend you utilize toloache in any of its forms. All that candle work we've been doing will be lost if you are accused of murder. Have faith that your petition will be heard and toloache will not be needed. When is the hearing?

The Santa Marta la Dominadora candle included in your kit needs to burn for seven days, be sure to start tonight. I have also included jabón Justo Juez for her to bathe with before her court date, and a Tapa Boca candle to silence her scheming brother-in-law. This is in addition to the Dume candle I am burning on Denise's soon-to-be-ex-husband. I brought in two spent Dume candles to show you all how much has changed since the beginning of the semester.

Yes, Leyla, *D-U-M-E*, not *D-O-O-M*. They are pronounced the same and, if used correctly, will have the same effect.
This solid black one is from when Denise and I first started working together, right after her most recent visit to the emergency room. All soot and ash. Who can tell me what that means? Correct. Obstacles. And this one, this one is from last week. See how the glass has only a pale gray shadow along the top rim? Now that the candle has burned clear, I am confident that with or without the court, Denise will finally see justice.

I would not call it that. Calling it *black magic* is devoid of context. I would call it *spiritual vigilantism* or *expedited karma*. Denise's soon-to-be-ex-husband has expended a significant amount of violent energy and accrued a bottomless psychic debt. Conversely, Denise has acquired a sizable cache of psychic credits she can spend without causing harm to herself or her loved ones. Denise, please raise your arm for the class to see. Thirteen stitches; she may balance the books any way she chooses.

I agree, Leyla. Spiritual vigilantism requires a proper class all its own. I submitted a proposal for a semester-length course but because your community college administrators have decided to invest your tuition in repaving the parking lot instead of your education, it is unlikely the class will be offered. And even if an advanced class is approved, I will only be accepting a limited number of students, specifically chosen by me. I am sorry, but none of you will be invited.

No, Viviana, that is not why. I know you are all intelligent and capable students. Intelligence and capability are not the issue. The issue is the cost. The darkness demands a payment that strips the protective layer of your spirit and invites pain and harm in unexpected manifestations. You might be emboldened by a flirtation with vengeful spirits to torture cruel men in their sleep the way they tortured you in yours. You may exchange favors with tricksters. Learn the language of demons. All of this is fine and fun until you fall in love with someone who does not love you. In fact, he despises you for what you did to his brother. Stubborn and impulsive, you might send reckless forces to rip him away from his beloved. Maybe you will force him to love you for all eternity. Maybe his devotion will curdle to dependence. Maybe all that time spent in his arms and under his gaze will feel like a cage and you'll dig your nails into his back hoping to pierce through his heart and, whoops, here come the three kids you didn't really want. Escape is found in strangers, in dancing across scuffed red floors with cheap Christmas lights overhead and amplifying your own power as you move your hands and hips all over Los

Angeles while he stays at home, caring for the hairless creatures you made together. Your children will despise you. They will grow up to be despised themselves. That will break your heart. His death will break your heart.

Your herbs won't fix it. The candles won't fix it. The polvitos and the blood won't fix it. Abandoned by your saints and demons, your most desperate petition will finally be accepted by a spirit more restless and wild than you. You'll be granted an opportunity for redemption by sharing your cursed knowledge with those in need, and providing shelter and affection to homeless and neglected cats. There's always a price for conjuring in darkness. You won't always know what it is until payment is due.

Now. What can you tell me about the Anima Sola?

Thank you, Javier. I can always count on you to do the required reading. The Anima Sola, that lonely soul chained to the bottom of purgatory surrounded by the eternal flames of her unrequited love, is the focus of your group project this afternoon. Before invoking the Anima Sola, understand that she is a powerful force to harness. She is the middle ground—not dark, not light. She strains her arms for salvation—not dead, not alive. She is permitted to make brief visits to our earthly world to inflict insomnia and obsessive thoughts on your lovers, enemies, and everyone in between. She is demanding. She is relentless. She will be with us soon.

Other questions?

No, you will never learn how to raise the dead, not even in the advanced class.

Security reasons, Leyla.

You are right, Viviana. While you cannot wake the dead, it is always important to honor them. Have you all been keeping up with your altars? Cleanliness and the disposal of offerings is important.

No, sir. We do not discuss that in this class. Spike, is it? Well, the answers you are looking for are found in a chemistry or anatomy class, but your instructors would find that line of questioning disturbing. Class is almost over, our time together is almost up. Let's have a look at your kit, yes?

Ah, you have the Gato Negro kit. Black cats are magnificent creatures and full of spirited energy. Class, this is a perfect opportunity for me to point out the folded-up sheet of paper that is included in everyone's supply kit. If any one of you is interested in learning more about black cats, please pay special attention to that form. I run the Behemoth Foundation, a black cat rescue group, and foster anywhere from four to a dozen stray black cats at any given time. If you would like to adopt a little panther for yourself or just want to volunteer for their care, please fill out the application included in your supply kit and return to me before the end of class. Be sure to indicate which days are best for an in-house inspection and sign your approval for a comprehensive background check.

I'm a widow, what's that got to do with anything?
That's a lazy stereotype; I rarely have more than a dozen cats in my house at one time.
Class, Mr. Spike's kit includes a Black Cat candle. Black Cat candles help us realize our wildest dreams and most intense desires.
Is that another attempt at a joke or a confession? I will remind you that our campus security is sparse but vigilant. Annalisa, put down the X-Acto. Viviana, stay close to Annalisa.

This kit also includes a bundle of sage to clear negativity and evil spirits. We also have a red blindfold, a black ball gag, and two industrial trash bags. Oh, look at this. You also have a small laminated portrait of Sinluz, one of my dearest companions. I found him in a rainstorm, wet, hungry, and trembling.

I ask you this as a kindness, Spike: Has anyone ever laughed at your jokes?
What's that supposed to mean?
You're out of line.
You need to calm down.
Calm down.
What's that in your hand?
Sit down!
Where'd you get that hook?

That wasn't in the supply kit! That wasn't in the supply kit!
Mujeres! The wire, the needles, the rope coiled around each of
your chairs.

Javier, bring me the toloache and mercury. Viviana, lock
the doors.

* * *

Open your eyes.
Unclasp your hands but remain in the circle.
Give yourselves a moment to readjust to the candlelight.
Deep breaths.

Class, you have all excelled in today's group project. I am
impressed by your precision and calm. Be proud of what we
have accomplished together. My vow to the Anima Sola is now
fulfilled. Your petitions paid. My gatos assured a feast. All
that is left for you to do is release your pigeons before sunset.
Be sure to truly want what you ask for, because you *will* receive
it. It will come in doses or in one rush of fortune, those are
things I can't tell you and you can't expect to know. There are
mysteries, there are mysteries.

Light your white candle before you fall asleep tonight and
wish the Anima Sola well on her journey, finally free and
untethered. She will remain sympathetic but not obli-
gated to attend to your needs. Grateful but not indebted.
Never attempt to summon the classmate who we've con-
demned to take La Anima Sola's place. No one can call him,

no one knows his true name. The instructor and I have an agreement.

I'll see you all when we return from spring break. Extra credit points for anyone who brings in cascarones.

Uncracked, Leyla. The eggshells definitely need to be uncracked.

No, Javier. Nothing to do with Easter. Or Ostara or the equinox.

Extra credit because cascarones are my favorite thing of this world. That satisfying *crunch* and the rainbow confetti polka-dotting the cement. All of us screaming and laughing and being sneaky without spite. Everything is possible and no one is afraid.

TIJUCA

Ada melted down her antique filigree necklace and a tangled knot of chains into a thin sheet of pliable gold. She hammered and molded the metal into a precise airtight cap that would seal off what remained of Armand's neck. The inside of her decapitated husband's head contained an avocado pit, orange seeds, kumquat peels, and dried tendrils of a passionflower vine. A poultice of fragrant lavender in the right eye, rose petals and honeysuckle in the left. Ada poured in sugar crystals to fill the remaining empty space of his skull. Finally, she pressed the gold cap against Armand's cold flesh, searing it shut. She wiped the flecks of dirt and sugar from her hands on an embroidered dish towel, and rubbed her knees, which ached from kneeling in her backyard garden for so long. She looked at her dead husband's face. The jade studs embedded in his ears glowed in the moonlight. Ada thought he resembled an oversized brooch, the kind a conquistador's wife might've worn to impress her friends. Tiny black hairs sprouted from the top of his bald head like on the belly of a pig. They prickled Ada's palms as she lowered him into her ostrich-skin tote bag.

Also inside her ostrich tote: a plastic baggie of dirt from Armand's hometown, his instructions, and an unframed family portrait. Their children had refused to see her off. They didn't attend the funeral, either. The last time they visited their father, the last time they tried to convince him his wishes were disgusting, maybe even illegal, Ada had sensed them silently appraising and claiming their dying father's belongings. Armand, one eye in this world and one in the other, had seen it, too. In a hoarse whisper, he instructed Ada to cut holes in all her silk scarves and nick all the crystal. *Everything else*, he said, *give away*. She wouldn't need any of those old things in their new home, the jungle was no place for antiques. Ada kissed his forehead and agreed, the jungle was no place for antiques.

Armand died after his merienda. Ada held his hand as he settled in for his afternoon nap. She knew he was gone when she felt his hand go limp and lose its warmth. As soon as Armand died, so did Ada the Wife. She was now Ada the Executor, executing her husband's instructions efficiently and accurately. First task on the list: call Tomás, the brujo/immigration attorney Armand had hired to guide Ada through the transition process.

Tomás arrived at the house just before sunset with a pair of girls clinging to his legs. "Mis nietas," he explained. "I couldn't leave them alone. They will behave." He gave them a look and they sat on the floor, quiet and still. After confirming Armand was dead, Tomás pulled a gleaming machete from his duffel bag. He handed the blade to Ada and said, "I'll wait for you outside."

As the streetlights flickered on, Ada and Tomás wrapped Armand's head with hoja santa and white petals before burying it in the backyard birria pit. While the head cured, Ada sat on her teal velvet chair and watched as Tomás and his granddaughters wrapped the headless body in white silk. She dug her fingers into the chair's soft fabric and felt a tickle of resentment in her throat. Armand wanted his head to be buried in the rich dirt of the Tijuca Forest surrounded by the fertile wild. Ada had promised she would stay with him there in the wild jungle until the end of her life and it was a promise she never intended to keep. Who would know?

Before boarding the plane to Brazil, Ada arranged for her teal chair and mahogany nightstand and the crystal champagne flutes and her mother's gold candle snuffer and one wardrobe case and one accessory case and two shoe cases and the boxes and boxes of photo albums to be transported to a condo in a thriving senior living community in San Diego. Her children could tear each other's hair out for everything else. Ada's new condo had a crescent-shaped balcony with an ocean view and the meals were certified organic. On Wednesdays, they had yoga.

Ada arrived in Rio de Janeiro just after sunrise. An air-conditioned private car picked her up at the airport. The driver gave his condolences but didn't ask any questions. Slowly, the car climbed up a hill through winding narrow roads lined with plywood houses and corrugated metal roofs. Ada craned her neck to peer at the towering soapstone Christ overlooking Rio. She followed the statue's gaze to see she was surrounded by infinite ocean and the charcoal shadows of mountains. Leaves and branches whipped across the car's steel body and windows when it turned onto an unpaved road. Ada closed her eyes to keep herself from getting sick. The driver took note and reduced the speed to a gentle roll.

After an hour of languid navigation through the dense

trees, the car stopped in front of a small brick house. Ada's leopard-print kitten heels sank into the dirt as the driver helped her out of the backseat. A sudden swarm of hot-pink butterflies flew up in front of Ada's face, temporarily blinding her. Ada wobbled on her heels and the driver effortlessly picked her up and carried her inside the house. He silently showed Ada the closets where her belongings were stored, the pantry full of food, the sprawling backyard jungle. He handed her the keys and kissed her cheek before turning to leave, closing the door behind him.

Ada was alone. The fourteen-hour flight, the anxiety of flashing the customs agents the hand signal taught to her by Tomás, the shock of everything going as planned. Her muscles twitched with relief. She set her bag on the wooden dresser and opened it to check on Armand.

His skin had gained a suppleness it never had when he was alive. Tomás said that might happen. She unfolded the instructions and drew a line through the tasks she'd completed. She then peeled the protective plastic off the bed's soft comforter and stretched out on the cool cotton sheets, sore and exhausted.

The following morning, Ada stood under the hot running water of the shower. It was covered in the same Talavera tile Armand had embedded in their kitchen floor. Ada let the water fall over the white roots of her dyed auburn hair until the heat ran out. She pressed her wet face against the cold hard tile, seeking the heartbeat of her husband. Humming a song she'd never heard before but recognized as the sound of her grief, she turned off the water and stepped out of the shower. She wrapped a thick navy towel around her body and, out of habit, dabbed perfume on her wrists and behind her ears before getting dressed.

The backyard was limitless. The sunlight beamed through a thicket of emerald leaves and the ground felt like a sponge underneath her feet. Following the instructions, Ada dug a two-foot hole in the backyard. *Don't you mean two-head hole?* Ada laughed at the joke her dead husband would never make. When she finished digging, Ada sprinkled the dirt from Armand's desert hometown into the earth. She held her husband in her lap and stared at his transformed face. She rubbed her thumb across his cheek. Her speckled hands looked like cracked pottery against Armand's rejuvenated flesh. Tomás warned Ada that true courage would be demanded right at this moment.

Customs, immigration, their dogs, none of that matters, Tomás said. *You are the greatest threat to your husband's final wish.* Ada the Wife felt her throat close up. The preparations and chaos of the journey were merciful distractions. Now, alone in the forest, under the scrutiny of the jungle's suspiciously silent birds, Ada imagined keeping him. Sleeping with him, talking with him. As long as she held him in her palms, he was still with her.

Ada pressed her lips against his forehead for a final kiss. Then, carefully, she peeled the hammered gold cap from Armand's neck. The heat was unforgiving. Immediately the flesh around his neck became gummy and his hair began to curl and clump. Ada felt the rigidity of his jawbone bowing under pressure from her fingers. Ada the Executor returned and she planted Armand's head in the earth, neck first. She shoveled the damp dirt over her husband's softening skull and packed it down flat with her hands.

The instructions were specific. Wait two weeks until traveling again. Ada the Widow was anxious to leave but knew her body wasn't ready for another long trip. She obeyed this last task without resistance, taking short walks into the jungle every morning before the rains came. She watched the capuchin monkeys chase each other and admired the spontaneous orchids that grew out of the sides of trees. She mistook a flamboyant spider for a flower and tried to pick it for her wooden nightstand. She suffered a swollen palm for half a day, having learned the lesson to not poke the jungle.

At the end of the first week, Ada noticed a skinny sprig of green where Armand's head was buried. The next day, the plant was as tall as Ada's knees and as thick as her fist. Ada postponed her flight for one week to see what would happen. The rapidly growing tree soon unfurled a branch with a bright purple flower. By the end the month, when her new condo in San Diego was fully prepped and waiting for her, the fragrant flowers attracted long-tailed hummingbirds and clumsy teal beetles. Ada delayed her flight another week. Then the fruit bats came. They feasted on the blossoming fruit. Ada wanted to understand what called all the creatures to the tree. She plucked one of the orange globes from a branch and bit into the fruit. She tasted mango and maracuya with the distinct aftertaste of Armand's cologne. Ada postponed her flight indefinitely.

Over the years, the tree grew as a sentinel over the small brick house. The trunk was a braided tower of textured bark and branches, bright flowers and sumptuous fruit. No matter how tightly the branches knotted and wrapped around each other, there remained a crevice in the gnarled trunk that the monkeys and birds avoided. Not even the spiders intruded. Ada loyally tended to the tree and the animals it attracted. She sat on the gnarled roots and braided her long white hair while the birds sang. She cooked with the fallen fruit and made teas with the speckled leaves, understanding she would be taken care of for as long as she lived, as long or as little as she wished.

The days and evenings began to blur into one another, and Ada could no longer ignore the pull of another world. Clothed only by the moonlight, Ada the Eternal stepped through the crevice into the mossy body of her tree. She nestled her face against its tangled softness and inhaled the sweet perfume of decaying mango and maracuya. The branches closed in around her.

TUNNELS

Tijuana

Epifania Fogata asked her sons questions no one could answer:

> *How many of our cures were lost in the conquests' fires?*
>
> *How many plants were burned to extinction?*
>
> *Do the ashes of your ancestors' codices contain methods for communicating with animals? With the dead?*

As they got older:

> *How many people still think you deserve to die?*
>
> *How many people will celebrate when you die?*

Before they each got married:

> *If you have children, will you also ask them these questions?*
>
> *If you have children, don't you want better for them?*
>
> *Don't you want to do something about this?*

Mama Epifania asked her son Arturo asked his wife Sofia asked their daughters who asked themselves: *Where* do we go from here?

Sugarland

Sofia Cortés was spared from the cotton fields even though her four-year-old hands were the ideal size to slip into the sharp-edged capullos and pull out the soft white fluff. Her father did not want his only daughter to become a hunchback. Instead,

Sofia worked in the kitchen, cleaning greens and sorting beans, helping to make meals for her family from the chicken her great-aunt whipped around her head like a lasso until its neck snapped.

Nha Trang

Arturo Fogata wormed his way through the blown-out earth, using his elbows and knees to push himself forward. When he was a kid, his brothers had called him Mico because of his monkey-like acrobatics. When he was an adult, his Army buddies referred to him as their pet Mexican rat. In the nightmares that followed him after the war, he became a chimera: a looming creature with flesh-tearing talons, a spindly prehensile tail, and collapsible bones digging his way through a rain-soaked cemetery with pyramid-shaped tombstones.

Xochimilco

The lush Floating Gardens were a short bus ride away from the Mexican university Sofia Cortés did not attend. Sofia's father waited a day after the scholarship letter arrived to repeat old stories that were wielded to fill young women with timidity. *The men will rape you, the jealous women will cut your pretty face.* Her mother and aunts rolled their eyes and insisted Sofia should go, leave the States and embrace an opportunity none of them would ever have. *He's just trying to keep you home. Don't listen to him. Don't let him scare you.*

Sofia leaned against the magnolia tree in her front yard and tried to divine her future in the wide petals of the white flower. She heard her mother yelling, and her father was uncharacteristically silent. Her brother, Lorenzo, had just announced he joined the Marines. Before the end of summer, he would board a bus to Camp Pendleton. Her brother's decision felt like an anchor tied around her feet. How could she leave her parents alone now? Sofia reluctantly declined the university scholarship and the Floating Gardens of Xochimilco.

When her brother returned from Vietnam, he convinced his family to move west. He said he'd found a place in Montebello that was perfect for them. *California is so much freer*, he promised. By the time they moved, Sofia had transformed an abandoned bathtub into a wildflower garden and learned how to propagate roses. Soon after arriving in East Los Angeles, she became Whittier Boulevard's flower girl. She spent her work hours listening to the Beatles and arranging roses and dahlias into lush sculptures, invoking the memory of a garden she had never visited.

East Los Angeles

Sofia ignored the shouts of her boss and stepped out to the sidewalk to get a closer look at the honking horns and massive march on Whittier Boulevard. She squinted to read the signs: *Tierra Y Justicia, our fight is in the barrio NOT vietnam! Chicano means POWER.*

Before Sofia could turn to grab the shop's camera, she heard a series of pops and screams. A man dressed in a camouflage jacket with a screaming eagle emblazoned on the sleeve slammed into Sofia with his eyes closed and his face twisted. *Me quemaron los ojos!* Recognizing the pained look Lorenzo would get whenever his mind wandered back to Vietnam, Sofia gripped the stranger's shoulders and held him steady against the wave of the now-panicked crowd. Carefully, she pushed him a few steps forward into the shop and ordered her cowering boss to lock the door.

Sofia sat on the floor and held the man's head in her lap, pouring cool water from a green plastic watering can over his eyes and face until his breathing calmed. When he finally opened his eyes, he said his name was Arturo Fogata. *Fogata, like a fire made of plants and trees.*

Water me.

Santa Ana

When their first daughter was a newborn, Arturo heard a faint and persistent scratching above the kitchen stove. After complaining about the noise to Sofia, who craned her neck to the ceiling but could not hear anything, Arturo dragged in a ladder from the backyard to investigate. Sofia gently placed a sleeping Celeste in her stroller for a walk around the neighborhood to give Arturo the quiet he needed as he searched for the noise. Arturo pinpointed the scratching in the attic—glorified crawl space full of itchy insulation, only one way in, one way out.

When Sofia and Celeste returned from their walk, all

the doors and windows were open and Sofia found her husband sitting in the living room staring at the wall, his face pale and wet. He told her he'd gotten trapped. He said that because everything was so dark, he didn't know what was left or right or day or night or city or jungle. When he heard his heartbeat echo in his ears like a desperate alarm, he decided to crawl backward, hoping that going in reverse would bring him to the edge of the attic door. If his foot dropped into an open space, he would survive, but until it did, he believed he would not. He said this while holding Celeste in his arms, rocking her back and forth and assuring himself he was home.

Undisclosed Location

The AeroSolar human resource department told Arturo Fogata that he was invited for a job interview because his last name tricked them into thinking he was a Japanese man. He waited for them to laugh but they didn't, so he clasped his hands together and rubbed one thumb over the other, a nervous habit he had developed in the trenches. He cleared his throat and began the interview on his own, making no attempt to mask his accent as he explained how to harness the power of the sun to create electromagnetic pulses.

Arturo stopped at a gas station on the way home from his interview. He picked up the pay phone and called his youngest brother. *I start on Monday*, he said. *Let's see where this goes.*

Santa Ana

Sofia paced in the living room waiting for Arturo's white hatchback to pull into their driveway. He was an hour late and wasn't picking up his office phone. Naima sat on the floor and colored all over the newspaper headlines, carefully shading the governor's face a deep red with yellow highlights. Sofia lifted the receiver and called the Fogata Landscaping Company.

Sofia worried Arturo had been taken in for a maquilla-jada. These violent makeovers had become a common detour for drivers who looked too dark or flat-nosed to be a real American. Instead of getting pulled over and harassed like in the early days of Proposition 187's passing, drivers were dragged into a nearby trailer for a disfiguring beat-down. She knew Arturo kept all his paperwork in his glove compartment: a signed proof-of-employment letter from AeroSolar, photocopies of his U.S. passport and DD 214, three years of tax returns, and car insurance. She also knew that paper could be ripped, burned, trampled under steel-toe boots.

Arturo arrived home three hours late with a busted lip and a limp right arm tied up in a sling he'd made out of his checkered work shirt. *I stopped at the gas station to get some Tylenol*, he explained to Sofia and his three brothers. *Those guys just wanted to make sure I'd have a reason to use it.*

Southern California

Sofia noticed the packs of coyotes darting behind the fruit vendor truck parked on the corner, hungry and uninhibited. Proposition 187 and its accompanying concrete border wall had disrupted natural migration patterns of hundreds of creatures, including bears, ocelots, and mountain lions. She'd seen this before, when her superstitious cousin couldn't see owls as anything beyond omens of death and shot dozens of them out of the sky with her pocket pistol. The rats quickly took over her grandmother's pantry and rivers of snakes writhed in their fields.

Sofia asked Arturo if AeroSolar had any drilling equipment. *I already have a garage full of microchips and magnets*, said Arturo. *Not going to risk bringing any equipment home.*

Sophia raised an eyebrow.

But, he continued, *my brothers might.*

The Fogata Landscaping Company soon began to build a vast network of subterranean roads under California's unending tangle of freeways. Moving the jaguars took years of careful planning.

Santa Ana

When Celeste was seven years old, Arturo Fogata showed her how to set up pigeon traps in their backyard. They'd prop a cardboard box up by one corner using only a twig from the avocado tree, then tie a string around the twig. Dry cat food was the bait. The pigeons swooped down and pecked around the trail leading to the trap. They always did a hesitant little dance when they reached the outer rim of the propped-up box. Arturo held his hands like a conductor and Celeste held the other end of the string, waiting for his cue. *Uno, dos, y . . .* he'd draw out the *y* until the curious bird took its place in the center of the trap. *Tres!*

They set every bird free. The point of the traps wasn't to collect pigeons. The point was to learn timing.

Nha Trang

Naima Fogata, Sofia and Arturo's restless second daughter, barely a high school graduate, decided to skip college and backpack across Southeast Asia. The Fogata Landscaping Company trucks lined the street and the smell of charred meat and fireworks hung in the air over the backyard barbecue. Naima gulped down Celeste's beer and walked toward the adult table, waiting for a lull in the conversation to loudly ask her dad if there was anything she should take with her when she visited Vietnam. Her uncles tensed as she rambled on about a documentary she'd seen about veterans who went back to the jungle to do a burial ceremony for the lives they'd taken—and for the parts of themselves now lost. She touched her hand to her heart and said she'd be happy to take something personal of his or bring something back if that would help him heal. Her dad said he had nothing to heal, he was *A-okay, baby*, and served himself another plate of ribs.

Westwood

Las hermanitas Fogata were raised to preserve and participate in their family's mission, but the way in which they interpreted their roles was entirely up to them. Naima—peroxided hair, shaved eyebrows, closet full of hot pink and neon blue—committed her life to multidisciplinary theatrics. Celeste, with the sense of duty and practicality usually embedded in eldest daughters, cast herself in the predictable and easily replicated Chicana template—political science degree from UCLA, Coyolxauhqui tattoo on her ankle, Anzaldúa quotes at the ready, and an unquestioned reverence for Frida Kahlo which she expressed anytime she wanted to irritate her sister. Celeste used to wear a brown beret, but buried it in her sock drawer after an ex-boyfriend told her it brought out the European in her face. Yet even at her most disruptive, leading high school walk-outs for showing Marlon Brando's *Viva Zapata!* during history class or writing passionate op-eds with lots of exclamation marks, Celeste's predictable protests were met with a predictable response: Everyone knew how to apologize, everyone knew how to loudly promise change without ever taking action. So while Naima had a tendency to be unreliable, Celeste lacked the flexibility to improvise, a trait her father considered necessary for survival. He'd say it like this: *Mija. You're going to bore us all to death.*

Chicago, Denver, San Francisco

The explosions occurred just as the sun set in the Pacific Ocean on Christmas Eve. One hundred and forty-seven dead in an attack coordinated by Save Our State terrorists. The slaughtered were undocumented—it would take years to accurately identify their remains and notify their families. A smaller explosion occurred at a nativity scene in Phoenix, but no souls were claimed. It was later determined to be an act of drunk teenage vandalism not related to the SOS-targeted Noche Buena bombings, yet the image of the bubbling plastic of the Virgin Mary's face become a symbol of national mourning to some, a declaration of war to others.

Santa Ana

Celeste and her fiancé, Mateo, spent New Year's Eve with her parents. Fireworks and bullets shot into the air to welcome in the chaotic new millennium.

We have to retaliate, said Mateo.

You don't know what you are saying, said Arturo. *This isn't a war.*

What else would you call that bombing? What would you call what they did to you at the gas station? What they do to our people every day?

A death rattle, said Arturo.

Sofia poured herself another glass of wine. *I think it's time for us to think about what* exactly *it is that we want to win.*

She looked at Celeste. *And what assets we might already have.*

Los Angeles

Generations of feral rock doves considered the central branch of the Los Angeles Public Library home, roosting in the abandoned eaves and above the barricaded doors. Once Celeste started her regular feedings, they welcomed her. Hundreds of birds would gather around her preferred bench and in a nearby tree, where they looked curious and out of place perched on the branches. Over time, Celeste gained the trust of nearly a thousand wild rock doves at the library.

Birds made Mateo uncomfortable. He grew up in Santa Monica and confided in Celeste that a pair of seagulls once attacked him over a bag of potato chips when he was a kid, which made her laugh until mascara ran down her face. So when Sofia asked her what Mateo thought of her plan, Celeste rolled her eyes and said that Naima had assumed the role of confidant, she'd even written a new play called *Quetzalcoatl* in honor of the pigeons. *Mateo doesn't like birds*, she said.

Sofia raised her eyebrow. *And I don't like weak men. Tell him he's going to help you or we'll have to consider him a liability.*

Santa Ana

On the one-year anniversary of the Noche Buena bombings, Arturo Fogata waited for a phone call from his daughter. Had she received the package? Did she understand the equations? Would she be able to make it work? Why was she taking so long to call? Sofia distracted him by giving him a present to open. He chose the one from his youngest daughter, a perfectly square package wrapped in newspaper. Inside, a card addressed to Mico signed by three of his surviving Army buddies, and a framed picture of his twenty-year-old body covered in dust and dirt, holding a tangle of wires in his hand, smiling.

Arturo stepped out to the sunlit front yard to pace. The dewy grass tickled his feet and a crow flew overhead. The construction was completed. His brothers said Celeste's idea would work. *Will it be enough?* He squinted as he looked up at the black birds cawing in the pine tree. A sudden flash of internal white light blinded him and brought him to his knees.

The Fogata women had time to say their goodbyes after the stroke. He was himself when they picked him up from the hospital, and he stayed semi-coherent through New Year's, but the doctors didn't know how long that would last. *I'm not going to drag it out*, Arturo promised. He had said that so many times before and reminded them once again: *Queridas, I'd rather be carne asada than a vegetable.*

Tijuana

His soul now inhabits the altar in Sofia's living room, and Celeste and Naima drunkenly tagged his name in the wet cement outside a downtown Santa Ana post office. After the cremation, the women each drove one of the Fogata Landscaping vans filled with precious cargo down to Las Playas to scatter Arturo's ashes. The Fogata brothers escorted the women out into the ocean on a cabin cruiser, far out enough to where the waves were so still they reflected the sky, but close enough to shore that they could see the flickering lights of the candles on the sand. Naima read a poem and Sofia gave the ocean a bouquet of gardenias and white roses. Celeste poured her father into the moon. The boat lolled atop the rippling waves. They each heard their name echoed in the laps of water. Celeste could clearly see him, smiling and clapping his hands: *Uno, dos. Uno, dos. Uno, dos, y . . .*

The Place Formerly Known as the United States of America

Sofia woke up at dawn. She walked past the empty vans and stacks of wire cages to join her daughters standing on the sand, looking to the sky. Gray feathers swirled in the sea breeze. They wouldn't be able to see the birds or hear the shouts and screeching of tires or the loud metallic crumple of cars from where they stood, safe from the northern chaos on the Baja beach. Yet they could close their eyes and imagine the loyal pigeons of the LAPL flying in formation over the Southwest, pulling a blanket of silence over the region. They envisioned the loyal library pigeons effortlessly emitting electromagnetic pulses from their powerful anklets, shutting down all the desperate 911 calls and any chance of a counterattack. The surviving Fogatas did not see any of this from the safety of the other side of the concrete border. They did, however, feel the earth rumble.

The sleek spotted jaguars roared as they burst through the ground, hungry and determined to reclaim their land.

ART SHOW

The Almost Philandering Fox
(East Gallery)

The Fox's wife prepared his lunch at dawn and brushed and braided her gray tail at twilight. But when her husband's tail brushed against the red pelt of the chemistry department's new professor, he did not pull away or apologize. Neither did the vixen. Their tails, and their eyes, kept meeting and lingering over each other's alert fur. The Fox lost sleep and sex, he spent his nights staring at the wall against the bed he shared with his trusting wife. He didn't fight off intrusive thoughts, he indulged in them, and became cranky whenever he was interrupted, always finding reasons to bare his teeth. *This*, he thought, *is infidelity*. He knew that touching the vixen would ruin his marriage, he knew ruining his marriage would ruin him. So he didn't touch the vixen or his wife and imprisoned himself in the limbo of love and lust for separate beings. He lost all sleep and sex until he found comfort in cutting out images of his daydreams, creating intricate dioramas of the emerald grass and fire-opal autumn trees of his native Kyoto.

A pop-up book of the Fox's haikus is available in the gift shop.

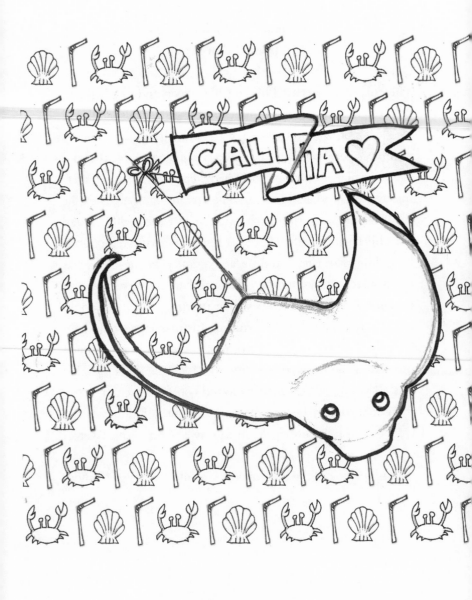

The Agoraphobic Bat Ray
(Courtyard)

After a failed attempt to become the California state bird, the defeated Bat Ray became paranoid and couldn't control his twitching tail in large crowds, always sensing an unseen threat. Convinced that he would not be able to live down the shame of his failed bid to become a state treasure, the Bat Ray began to question his god as to why he was born with wings to soar through the swaying kelp beds and salty water. He took a vow of silence and committed himself to learning the history and struggles of his species. The Bat Ray's introspection empowered him to overcome the dread of defeat, and his steady intake of prose written by and about bat rays illuminated a path to unwavering self-love.

The Bat Ray is collecting signatures for his third campaign for California state bird. The petition is available at the exit, next to his assemblage of discarded campaign buttons.

The Polyamorous Cat
(West Gallery)

The Cat has multiple lovers in the neighborhood, families and individuals who feed her and pet her soft head. She is unable to commit to any of their homes. The collars, the catnip mice, the Fancy Feasts, the velvet-lined beds, none of these fill the need she can't define. *This is my nature*, she tells them with her tail flicks. *I can't love you forever*, she says through purrs, and to drive the point home, she leaves as suddenly as she arrived.

Watercolors, with their seeping and sprawling properties, have become the Cat's preferred medium. She paints in all colors, pursuing an "effect" rather than an "image." A boxed variety set of her greeting cards is available in the gift shop.

Insert self-portrait here.

The Angry Rooster
(West Gallery)

The Rooster's inability to fly caused him great psychological pain. Nightmares tortured him, nightmares in which he was an eagle soaring high over his backyard wire coop. He often woke up crowing hours before dawn. His hens have raw spots on the back of their heads from his constant pecking. At their insistence, the Rooster reluctantly enrolled in restorative art classes, desperate for relief from his impotent wings.

Each canvas is a snapshot of his evolution—the furious paintings of oily red slashes and violet splatters of his early work give way to the mellow green pointillism of his meditative landscape period. The soft blue skies with bright yellow whorls are the work of a Rooster transformed. The Rooster is one of the founding members of the Gallo Art Collective, and his latest project is mixed-media collage exploring the theme of "Dirt." In his free time, he volunteers teaching motherless chicks how to draw.

The Rooster's paintings are on loan from a private collector. The Rooster challenges you to a self-portrait.

"Sugar Pyramid"
(Sculpture Garden, see show times)

This performance art piece by experimental troupe Colibris Before Columbus challenges and confronts the objectification and exotification of hummingbirds. After three years of collecting stories from a variety of peer species including the Anna's, Rufous, Violet-Crowned, and Broad-Tailed, the Colibris created a pointed response to society's treatment of hummingbirds as "adorable birdies," and the deliberate erasure of the birds' warrior past.

Warning: This is an interactive performance. One member of the audience will be sacrificed each night. Absolutely no photographs allowed.

The Paranoid Peacocks (Basement Level)

The repentant and reformed members of the True Blue Movement are permanent artists-in-residence. Escapees from the infamous True Blue compound, the Peacocks are reminders of the dangerous tendency of fauna to follow maniacal leaders. Although the escape liberated them from their vows of selective silence (*The only truth is the truth of blue / Speak blue, listen blue, protect blue / Keep the feather pure*), the Peacocks suffered a prolonged period of shock where they could not communicate beyond cryptic messages scratched out on the basement floor. When they first arrived at the gallery, the Peacocks maintained the same disciplined daily routine that made the True Blue Movement so terrifying, starting with a morning ritual of gathering in a circle to pluck the brilliant plumes off their comrades. Multiple attempts to distract the birds from their mutilation (dance therapy, face-painting, jazz) failed.

After exactly one year of silent residence, the Peacocks fanned the skinny white remains of their bare tails and began to shriek. They have not stopped. To avoid exhaustion or damage to their vocal cords, they take shifts. When asked why they screech, the off-duty Peacocks respond that they have heard the ghostly songs of the woodpeckers and pigeons. Of the blue jays. Of their own, the peacocks. Their compulsive cries are a penance for remaining silent for so long.

Recordings are not available at the gift shop, neither are earplugs.

CLAP IF YOU BELIEVE

I saw Satan at the train station. The platform for the south-bound train was crowded: clusters of Mexigoths, a paletero man leaning against his cart, an older man mouthing the words of the *Los Angeles Times* as he read. I noticed all of them without looking at them directly—don't you ever look at them directly—but when he appeared, I broke my rule and stared. He wore a charcoal-gray suit made of thin material, Goodwill's finest, and crooked round glasses. He looked at me and scratched his nose with a thick yellow nail. The wiry black hair on his finger grew beyond his top knuckle. I reached into my pocket for my eye drops and squeezed them into my left eye. I closed them and counted to three. When I reopened them, he was still there, humming what sounded like "Lucy in the Sky with Diamonds" but not quite. He sneezed and I smelled Jägermeister. I knew he was the Devil because it was a clear sunny day and his shoes were olive-green galoshes.

When I arrived in Santa Ana, I hopped off the Amtrak onto the terra-cotta-tiled walkway that led to the parking lot. The shouting train horn drowned out the garbled station's loud-speaker as it announced the time. It was just before noon, I could tell by the way the sun felt on my skin. A pair of mourning doves made a nest on the dried-out top basin of the empty fountain near the train station's entrance. I sat on the circular ledge and again took out the vial of eye drops from my back pocket. The medicine rolled off the side of my face like tears and I wiped them away just as my dad's beige Volkswagen sputtered and gasped its way to pick me up. He leaned over to open the door and asked, "How did it go?"

I shrugged. "It's too far. I don't want to take the train to L.A. every day."

"There are probably art galleries around here that are hiring. What about that car museum? Maybe they'll let you drive a Ferrari."

I wiped off my lip gloss with the back of my hand, leaving behind a glittery sheen on my bruised knuckles. "Yeah, maybe."

Stopped at a red light on the way to Polly's Pies, I stared at the precariously balanced Cube a short distance away. The Cube, a giant six-sided man-made wonder located at the Discovery Science Center covered in amorphous silicon modules that convert solar energy into electricity. From where I sat in a trembling 1960s automobile, the towering black cube looked like an artifact from an unattainable future. I stared at it, the sun's reflection a circle of glowing white light atop millions of solar cells. The white light stretched and expanded across the Cube, taking the shape of a woman. A moment before the light turned green, the Virgin Mary appeared against the black background, a glare of silver her incandescent halo.

———

The waitress cleared away our ketchup-smeared plates and replaced them with slices of pie. I figured seeing the Virgin on the Cube was some sort of Mexican rite of passage I had finally achieved and told my dad. He said he saw La Virgen on a pizza. "I'm serious, Apá," I said.

"So am I," he said.

I swirled the straw in my Coke, making it a point not to smile.

"What did she look like?" he asked. "Like the Virgen de Guadalupe?"

"She had her arms open and light shooting out of her palms."

"Cómo Iron Man?"

I nodded.

"Ah. Pues. Ya te agringaste. Good thing your tía Amalia is in town. She'll fix that for you."

I laughed and we ate our dessert in silence.

He wiped his mouth after finishing his pecan pie, then wadded up his napkin into a ball. He rubbed the fading letters of my grandma's name inked on his knuckles, then pointed to the purplish spots on my hands. "You're going to help me patch up those holes in the garage tomorrow."

I tucked my hands under the table and nodded.

"Have you talked to your mom about it yet?"

I twisted the cap off my eye drops and tilted my head back. Closed my eyes and counted to three. "No."

"Another one of those books came in the mail. You should talk to her."

Forgive & Forget? An Exploration of Closure Culture.
Finding (and Losing) Your Self Through Meditation.
Chakras & Chia Seeds: Recipes for Healing.

The living room had a shelf dedicated to books my mom wanted me to read. I had conceded to listening to her summaries of the titles, nodding and *mm-hmm*ing as she worked her way through her inner labyrinth of guilt. My mom and I share a nightmare. It involves a car, a house with barking dogs, and a scorching sun. I'm the one who has the memory, yet her nightmares are worse than mine. "This isn't your fault," I would say after she finished her latest book report. And each time she would just nod and look away.

Two truths and one lie:

1. La Mariposa Morfo Azul (the blue morpho butterfly) is valued for its remarkable bright blue iridescence and magnificent wingspan that measures over three feet upon first unfurling from the chrysalis.

2. La Mariposa de la Muerte (Butterfly of Death) is not really a butterfly, but a moth. Its actual name is the Black Witch Moth and it is identifiable by the number nine imprinted on its forewing, the same number that is associated with the Yoruban deity Oya, Queen of the Cemetery.

3. La Santa Muerte (Saint Death) is the post-Conquest incarnation of Mictecacihuatl, Aztec Goddess of the Underworld. She is invoked in secret rituals in places that have minimal light. She is often referred to as the inverse of the Virgin Mary. She is the one you go to for things you can't ask your mother.

My aunt Amalia is the one who taught me the power in keeping secrets. She also taught me how to use lemon to lighten my hair, how to bathe in honey and rum to pull the attention of my hot biology teacher who never remembered my name. How to tell a convincing lie: *Think of a clear blue sky.* My mom worried I wanted to grow up and be Amalia, willowy and strange and unafraid. My dad stayed out of their way, especially when they argued about me. The only time he tried to defend his sister, my mom locked him out of the bedroom for three nights.

Their last blowup was when Amalia arrived unannounced from Mexico City to convince me to withdraw my application for the junior espionage program. The CIA once had its version of child stars, little ethnically ambiguous teens they planted all over the world for intelligence recon. They had a recruitment booth at my high school summer job fair and convinced me that I deserved to see the world and learn how to make my invisibility work for me. Amalia threw her studded black leather purse onto the living room table and demanded to know why I was enrolling in a program so stupid and dangerous. She compared me to both a cow and a chess piece, then clicked on my dad's old stereo and turned up the oldies station so *they* couldn't hear her as she ranted about COINTELPRO and Operation Condor with "Baby Love" playing at full volume. I am sure that my mom agreed with her, because it *was* stupid and dangerous, but she put up a fight in my defense. Maybe she was tired of Amalia trying to claim me, or she wanted to antagonize my dad into speaking up. Maybe she really believed the recruiter, that it was a military-enhanced study abroad specifically tailored for underperforming yet high-potential high school students, and that it would help me discover a possible future. The next day, my mom signed off on all my paperwork and lent me to the United States government.

The night before my flight to Miami, my mom and dad went to church while Amalia rubbed a live white dove and bright green ramas over my body. It was an easy backyard ritual, a spiritual exfoliation, and my only responsibility was to set the bird free without touching its body. Doing so would reinfect me with my discarded spiritual toxins and invite tragedy and misfortune, according to my aunt. *Mala suerte*, she said while holding my face in her hands and searching my eyes for signs of weakness. I walked over to the park down the street, carrying the dove in a crumpled brown paper bag. I gently shook the bird out of the bag onto the carved-up wooden picnic tables, and it steadied itself on the etched initials and sigils. Instead of soaring into the lilac canopies of the jacarandas, the bird flew low and dizzy, straight into a neighbor's front lawn. A skinny orange tabby skulked into view. My shouts and claps did nothing to prevent it from pouncing. I seized the cat and forced open his jaw, holding the shocked dove in my hands. A smattering of red flecks on its white feathers, a looseness in its neck, and a violently beating heart. I carried the bird back to the park and kept it company until the sky turned dark and the night residents claimed their spaces in the grassy field.

Amalia waited for me on the edge of my bed, tapping the toes of her black leather riding boots on my packed suitcases. As I reported the bird's condition between life and death, Amalia's eyebrows twitched and furrowed. She crossed her arms over her chest and said, *You are someone's prey.* Her black nails dug into her own flesh. *How bad do you want to do this CIA shit?* she asked. *It's my destiny,* I answered. She then brushed a bundle of rosemary over my body and burned the herbs in one of my mom's aluminum pasta pots. Amalia traced the curling smoke with her fingers. *Yeah,* she said. *It is.*

A few days after I'd landed in-country for my first assignment, my mom found a dead dove on her porch. She called Amalia immediately, finally validating my aunt's expertise with the occult. Amalia then confessed what she had kept hidden even from me. She had done all she could to protect me from what she sensed was waiting for me on the other side of the equator. I wouldn't come back the same, she reassured my mom, but I'd come back. As long as I was willing to eventually pay the price.

My assignment was somewhere in the Mercosur bloc, I am not authorized to say exactly where. I collected local newspapers, learned slang, and studied television shows to pick up on body language and evolutions in topical humor. I'd then send reports and clippings disguised as enthusiastic handwritten letters "home." My group added a critical dimension to understanding the local human climate. We captured what was missed by the hidden cameras. We were cheaper than satellite surveillance, easier to replace, too. But unlike those fleshless computers in the sky, we were highly visible. Sixteen-year-old me liked to eat chicharrones and drink imported Jack Daniel's straight from the plastic bottles like all the other yanquis. I liked to style my long hair over my left eye and wear an intentionally painful lip gloss that stung like venom, making my smile pink and puffy. I did these things for me, for that thrill that radiated out of my navel when I looked at myself in the streaky bathroom mirror of our safe house. I did it for me, but the three men who shoved me into the backseat of their Mercedes thought I did it for them. My lemon-lightened hair, my yellow crop top, my wobbly walk. If I showed you the official report of what I can only refer to as my "car accident," it would be pages and pages of black lines with a scattering of intriguing but meaningless phrases like *shopping mall parking lot, barking dogs, broken window, Charles Bonnet*.

I'd listed Amalia as my primary emergency contact. She boarded a plane from Mexico City and arrived at the clinic the morning after I'd stumbled my way back to the safe house. Her black T-shirt was tucked tightly into her skinny black jeans and her smudged eyeliner settled in the creases below her yellow eyes. Gata, my dad's family called her. When I was ten years old, she held my hand and asked me in a high-pitched voice to please stop calling her Tía Gata. She wanted me to call her Amalia. She believed the more people who loved her and said her name out loud, especially children, the more power she could accrue. This is around the time my mom started dropping her voice anytime Amalia came up in conversation, as if her sister-in-law could listen through walls and across the continent to hear the scorn in her voice.

The internal investigation was scheduled right there in the medical examination room. I sat in a pilly lavender hospital gown that felt too warm against my purpling skin. My aunt leaned against the door of a medical supply cabinet, tapping a cigarette against the thick copper cuff around her wrist. A blonde in an indigo suit and mandatory U.S. flag pin took photos of my face and tape-recorded the interview. I could barely form sentences. Amalia almost immediately interrupted her questioning: "It wasn't her fault."

The patriot violently nodded her head and agreed. "Of course it's not her fault. We require a comprehensive understanding of the circumstances to identify how this type of incident could potentially be avoided in the future."

"Mass castration?"

The blonde blinked twice, then pursed her lips.

Amalia crossed her arms over her chest and rolled her eyes. "As if you people never've done anything like that before."

That was three years ago. Every year since then, I've owed a soul for the life I was allowed to keep. This was my last chance to balance the scales my aunt tipped in my favor.

* * *

After I finished listening to my mom's discourse on the healing power of chia seeds, I borrowed my dad's Bug and visited Amalia at the stylish hotel she usually stayed at, near the edge of Santa Ana, away from the constant construction noise of our downtown and right down the street from Noguchi Garden. Part of my mom and Amalia's truce was that my parents would pay for her hotel anytime she visited. Even when she went out of her way to pick out the most expensive suite with all the add-ons, it worked out better for everyone. I knocked on her hotel door with a carton of white eggs under my arm, ready to pay my debt.

Amalia was already wading in the underworld when I arrived. She opened the door, silent except for her monotone humming. Our embraces and catch-up conversations would come after. She pulled back her black hair into a bun; a hidden streak of white split her skull in two. Amalia continued humming as she set up candles and bundles of leaves and bowls of water around the sink and in the bathtub, transforming the hotel bathroom. I cleared a space on the tiled floor, folding the towels into neat squares as Amalia pantomimed instructions. When I'd set the floor to her liking, she handed me a thin notebook and a pencil. We sat cross-legged on the folded towels, lighting the candles that encircled us. Between us was a Tupperware container half filled with something creamy and sweet. I smelled coconut milk and clove. The other ingredients I couldn't figure out and knew better than to ask. Amalia repeatedly rubbed an egg on my head and cracked it into the milky mixture. After a few of the eggs were cracked, my aunt shook a small olive-green vial in my face.

"What's that?"

"Accelerant," she said. Amalia squeezed a few drops on her

tongue and fluttered her eyelids, the whites flashing like strobes. A swift and silent presence seeped in through the ceiling and filled the room with its underwater quiet. The overhead sensor light clicked off and she fully descended into another world.

"Picture yourself on a train at the station," she said in a low growl. In the shadows of the candlelight, her face and her voice were no longer hers. She opened one eye and bared her teeth in a lopsided smile. "There you are." She started humming again, louder this time, and the sound began to form a recognizable melody. Sweat from the rising candle heat made the fabric stick to my skin. I remained still and focused on my aunt, watching her sway side to side like a pendulum, whispering and watching me with one eye. She stopped moving and looked up at the ceiling, reciting names I didn't recognize. She repeated them again, slower than before, and I hurriedly scribbled them in the notebook. She faced me once again and spoke in a gasp. "Three years." She pressed her finger into the iris of her open eye, now a solid white. "You owe me. Send me to them. Send me to feed." Amalia reached out for both of my hands and gripped them tightly over the plastic container, her thick nails digging into my knuckles until they bled. Drops of my blood fell into the container and Amalia threw open her arms as if she were about to take flight, knocking the candles over, their wax spilling across the tiled floor. The overhead lights flickered on and Amalia's limbs flailed as she fought her way back into her body. She scrambled into the bathtub and I held her steady by the neck and turned on the water. Drenched and laughing, Amalia returned.

———

Her hair wrapped in a towel, Amalia came out of the bathroom with the offering, now covered with a red Tupperware lid and a thick bundle of leaves. She sat next to me on the queen-sized bed and muted the TV.

"Bury this in your backyard, close to decaying fruit." She carefully placed the Tupperware in a perforated Adidas shoebox. "And these." She held the bundle of lime-green leaves under her nose and inhaled. "These are from deep in the Amazon." I took a deep breath. They smelled like black licorice. Amalia laid the rama over the Tupperware and I noticed pale white buds clinging to the stems. "The sooner you get this in the ground, the better." The sky was orange when I left Amalia's hotel room with a shoebox full of offerings and a deep purple candle, the names of my prey folded neatly in my pocket.

On my way home, I found a church with a covered parking lot. The familiar smell of pine and copal was immediately comforting. I tucked my purple candle under my armpit and made my way to the alcove of petitioners' candles. I walked the length of the church, unable to break the childhood habit of making the sign of the cross as I passed the altar, forgetting the choreography and starting at my belly button and ending up somewhere in hell. The crowded tiers of candles flickered in the darkened corner, each flame meant to bring peace to their petitioners. I wasn't cold but I held my hands over their fire. I decided I also deserved the peace, even if it meant delivering chaos. I don't know who I'd be if those men in the Mercedes hadn't interfered. That version of me doesn't exist, there is no reason to wonder about or mourn her. That didn't mean I couldn't avenge her. I ran my thumb over the talon of the owl and sinewy muscles of Death imprinted on the candle Amalia had given me. I set the candle in an empty space between the white votives and struck a match. It snapped and I smelled sulfur. I lit the wick. Rotting teeth disintegrating in putrid mouths, blistering eruptions on skin, suffocating in an all-consuming house fire—these are the things I imagined as I burned the paper in my candle's hungry flame.

Staring at the flame in the dark church fucked with my eye in a way I wasn't prepared for. I drove slowly, unable to recognize the street names or make sense of the blurring traffic lights. I parked crookedly in front of my parents' house, relieved to have arrived. Kneeling at the base of the orange tree in their backyard, I brushed aside the decaying fruit and scooped out the soft dirt using only my hands, making a cantaloupe-sized hole. I opened the shoebox and almost didn't recognize the leafy green bundle Amalia had given me. I carefully lifted the now-dried-out branch. Wide brown leaves dangled from the stems, the edges polka-dotted with black-and-white spots. I quickly poured the contents of the Tupperware into the hole. The eggy cream seeped into the graves of deceased family cats and their murdered birds. I packed the dirt over the coconut offering and crowned it with the thick bundle of Amazonian leaves. I stepped back and brushed off the dirt from my hands. I turned around and jumped a little, surprised to see my mom in a gray tracksuit and running shoes, standing next to the white garden bench, watching me. I didn't know how long she'd been there.

She sat on the bench and raised her eyebrows, fanning herself with a lime-green pamphlet.

I looked at the crescent moon and squinted. Sometimes I thought I could see the tongues of fire on its surface. *Streamers and floaters*, the ophthalmologist called them, a nonstop ocular party.

"Do you believe in curses?" I asked.

"You think you're cursed?"

I looked at the pile of soft dirt. "Not anymore."

I sat next to her and took the pamphlet from her hands. "*Absent Mindfulness*," I read aloud. "Does this really help you?"

She folded her arms over her chest. "A little." She pointed to the pile of leaves. "Does Amalia help you?"

"She said she wants to see you before she goes home."

My mom clucked her tongue and rubbed her arms. A weak breeze rustled the orange tree leaves. Crickets, the distant echo of a late-night party, murmurings of our neighbor talking to someone outside on the phone. We sat together breathing in and out in the twilight. Soon our breath was all I could hear. The leaves of the dried-out branch that Amalia had included in my offering began to twitch and crinkle. We both held our breath and listened. And at that moment a flurry of brilliant morpho butterflies broke through their chrysalises and spiraled up around the orange tree and into our backyard. They fluttered toward us and landed on our heads and hands, their deceptive brown wings expanding to reveal the chaotic iridescence within. I closed my eyes and counted to three. I knew the morphos were real because when I opened my eyes, a butterfly settled on my mother's open palm, her smile a revelation.

MOKSHA

My sister, Cora, and I walked the malecón hunting for something to do. We cut through clouds of patchouli and speakers playing tinny cumbia, passing rickety kiosks selling straw hats and miniature carnivorous plants. We were steps away from the wooden pier when Cora jerked to a stop and gasped. "Ohmygod, Chelo. Look." I followed her gaze to a lurching pale figure in the middle of the walkway. Cloaked in a frayed polyester tuxedo, he wore a plastic top hat faded by the sun, and rivulets of bright red blood stained the corners of his frozen smile. Stabbed through his chest, a splintered wooden crucifix stained with a glue halo where the plastic Jesus used to be. The sign around the cross read: *Museo de las Chupasangres*.

Cora hooked her arm in mine and led me toward the museum's entrance. "This is going to be awesome," she promised. I pulled back a little, hoping to instead look for the man with the gigantic green and pink parrot. We'd seen him walking the pier yesterday afternoon right around this time, but there was too much of a crowd around him to get close enough for a picture. The only souvenir I wanted, I told my parents, was a picture next to that monstrous bird. Cora narrowed her eyes at my resistance and tugged harder. "C'mon. It won't take long." I gave in and fished out a couple of pesetas from my pocket.

We dropped our coins in the turnstile and entered the makeshift museum's narrow hallway. Red velour hung limply from the wooden walls and tattered pieces of taped-together construction paper served as exhibition placards. The museum was no bigger than the lobby of our hotel, with red tape arrows on the floor guiding us forward. Cora tapped her blue fingernails against a plastic case full of skulls.

"Kitschy," she said. Most of the skulls had belonged to adults, but there were some the size of my fist. All had elongated and serrated canines. "Imagine having to live like that," Cora said, and rubbed her jaw in sympathy.

We smirked at the movie posters of girls worshipping chiseled and brooding chupasangres. We made faces in the trick mirrors that gave us holographic fangs. We bowed our heads in reverence to the bronzed bat statue commemorating the Matanza de Murcielagos. Thousands of innocent bats were slaughtered, back when the slayers believed chupasangres could shape-shift and fly. There was a little TV playing an amateur documentary about the fallout of the massacre, detailing the eventual outlawing of the slayers. Cora dismissed it by saying it was basically the same one we'd seen a hundred times at school back home, but we both knew that the official version left out all the good parts like the Bleed Out! protest marches, and the ugly Citizen-Slayer campaign that encouraged civilians to violently defang their neighbors. Our parents had told us to ignore what school taught, that we could ask Tío Julio anything we wanted to know. He had been an activist during those years and was arrested a couple of times fighting against Senate Bill V666. He even almost married a chupasangre! But he had a problem with commitment and refused couples therapy, so, like all his other girlfriends, she got tired of his shit and left him.

"Chelo!" Cora shouted. I reluctantly pulled myself from the revolting uncensored footage of the bat bonfire and caught up to her. I watched as she traced her fingers over a flaky portrait of a woman with a painted blue face. "It's La Duende!"

Portraits of La Duende never looked anything like La Duende, the ancient pop singer who both my mom and grandma, and *her* grandma, worshipped when they were teenagers. No one agreed on what she looked like because no one ever saw her the same way.

"This is during her Eastern Mystic phase," Cora said. "Right before she went nuts."

La Duende's exhibit consisted of a wall full of laminated photocopied images of the artist doing her signature half-lunge pose and bared-fangs snarl. In one photo, La Duende wore a colorful feathered headdress and held her hands over her head like little cobras poised to strike—her Rio Carnival phase. Another picture with a feathered cape and neon-green monokini—her Birds of the Amazon phase. The photo with the thick braids showed La Duende at the height of her Rope phase. And that one there, with the pieces of bread glued to an aluminum foil hat, my favorite, her Electric Toaster phase.

"Why did La Duende go nuts?" I asked.

Cora turned out her feet and slowly bent her knees. My sister had to plié or tendu every couple hours out of suspicion that if she didn't, her body would suddenly lock up and stop obeying her. "Some people say it's because she ran out of phases.

Her fans always wanted something new and she couldn't keep up with technology. It's not like the old caveman days when she could just wait until they died out and then repeat her act for the next generation. YouTube killed that trick."

I nodded. La Duende in her Steampunk Clown phase, La Duende in her droll Edwardian Gentleman phase. La Duende as a box of crayons.

"But I don't think that was the only thing. I think she sort of lost touch with herself when she got into her Mystic phase."

"What do you mean?"

"Death is a lie, Chelo. The mystics taught her that we always come back after we die, just in different bodies."

"But La Duende couldn't die."

"She couldn't be *killed*," my sister corrected me. "Only dying by the hand of their true love can a chupasangre's immortal soul be restored."

"Says who?

"It's in the *Vampire Watcher* series. That's how Lulubella and Rodrigo finally end up being together."

"That's a dumb novela!"

"Based on *fact*. How else can you explain why La Duende stabbed herself? She was her only true love. Stabbed herself right through the heart." My sister plunged an invisible knife into her chest and rolled back her eyes. "She was ready for a new body. A new life. Who knows where she is now?"

We turned the corner and the outside light filtered in through the exit door's square glass window. I reached my hand out to turn the handle when Cora gripped my shoulder to stop me.

"Look," she whispered. I followed her eyes to a sleek obsidian dagger hanging on the wall above a display showcasing replicas of La Duenda's diamond-studded fangs. An embedded heart-shaped ruby shimmered on the dagger's handle.

"It's just like La Duende's!" She looked around to make sure that we weren't being watched.

"Cora," I said under my breath. She would never become a famous dancer, but her ballet training made her an excellent thief. Before I could stop her, she rose up on her toes, swiped the dagger, and leapt past me toward the exit. I pivoted and ran out behind her, following her down the pier toward the water until we were far enough from the crowds.

We leaned against the splintery railing and angled our bodies into a V so people couldn't see what we had in our hands. The deep teal of the calm ocean peeked through the warped wood under our feet. We took turns admiring the knife. "It's really sharp."

"Duh, it's obsidian," Cora said.

"Everything in that museum was plastic."

Cora's eyes widened. "But it could be La Duende's actual dagger. Look at that. Touch that. That's real obsidian."

"It's not her dagger."

"La Duende was for the people. I bet you anything she left dozens of these, hundreds, all over the world." She looked out into the expanse of the sea and pointed the tip of the dagger to the horizon. "I bet you she put all her memories into hundreds of these knives so when she's out there and living in her new body, she'll find one of these no matter where she ends up and remember everything."

"Things don't have memories, Cora."

"*Everything* has a memory. You just have to know how to ask for it." Cora held the knife in her right hand, poised to stab something. "Give me your hand."

I knew that look in her eye. It was the look that could convince our parents to let her spend the night at a friend's house, a look that could trick those friends into crashing a loud backyard party none of them were invited to. The same look she'd given me the next morning when she showed me the marks on her neck and asked me to forge our mom's signature for an emergency dose of Plan V. I knew that the same wide-eyed look was a prelude to a riot if she didn't get her way. So I held out my hand and Cora smiled, my reward for not putting up a fight. My sister drew the blade across my skin, a short line just below my pinkie. Little beads of red. When it was my turn, I sliced a line across her palm. A clumsy burgundy slash. We clasped hands and each said our name, then each other's name. To close the improvised ritual, we licked our palms and spit into the ocean. "Now we'll be sisters in the next life, too."

We stayed at the end of the pier, listening to the waves and straining to hear the voice of a once immortal pop star, summoned by our blood on the knife. When I opened my eyes, the feathery clouds in the sky had turned a deep pink. The man with the giant parrot—*It was just a stupid puppet anyway*, Cora would later say at the airport to stop me from sulking—was nowhere to be seen. My only vacation souvenir would be an itchy cut on my hand. "They wanted us back at the hotel before sunset," I said. "You know how Mom gets when we have to pack."

Cora took a deep breath and opened her eyes. "Okay," she said. "I don't think we should keep this." She looked at the dagger and pressed her fingertip against its point. Her palm had stopped bleeding, but the dried blood covered her wrists. "It's not ours, you know? What if La Duende comes looking for it?"

"What are we going to do with it?"

Cora looked down at the waves and handed me the knife. "You do it. Make a wish. Just don't be tosca with it. Toss it in gently so you don't kill any fish."

I dropped the obsidian into the ocean. It barely made a splash.

To get back to the hotel, we had to walk against the tide of tourists making their way to the edge of the pier to witness the legendary green flash of the seaside pueblito. On our first night of vacation, our tour guide had said if we made a wish at the moment of the green flash, it would come true within the year. I wished to finally have my own room and my sister wished for men to find her irresistible. Both of us would unfortunately get what we asked for. We jutted our elbows out and pushed against the crowds, looking up at the tourists' salt-water-brined faces, which picked up the orange and pink hues of the moody sky. My sister and I leaned on each other as we walked against their fleshy mass. "Do you think any of them are chupasangres?" I whispered.

"No," she said. "But we could be."

We slipped off our scrunchies and narrowed our eyes.

We *prowled* the malecón.

The crowds pulled away from us, such satisfying flashes of

shock in their eyes. Cora suddenly stopped and pointed at the air. "Ssh. You hear that?"

I tilted my head to listen. Next to the now-darkened Museo de las Chupasangres, a luchador mask vendor's boom box emitted a low husky voice.

"It's La Duende!" Cora clapped. "This song, it's from her Viva Las Vegas phase." She closed her eyes and swayed, humming along to the music. She then shot her arms straight up over her head and gnarled her hands like claws. She stomped her right foot forward and froze in position. "C'mon, Chelo," she whispered. I clapped and stomped my feet, striking a pose and snarling. I mimicked her. She was my older sister, I always mimicked her. Even now when I visit her grave, I lie flat and still with my arms at my sides and tell her she's not missing much and ask her why she still hasn't sent me a postcard from her latest life. On the malecón, I mimicked her. I twisted my torso and scratched at the air. We demanded the attention of the tourists passing by, lunging and growling and snapping our teeth at pale-faced babies until they cried.

When those tourists talk about their vacation, they remember us, my sister and me, seething and contorting down the malecón. And because time dulls the gray moments of life and only the most vibrant colors remain, the tourists see only the truth of who we are and will always be: jagged wet teeth and lacy brick-red bracelets adorning our brown wrists, clawing and biting, as bodiless and immortal as the waves.

BURIAL

The windows vibrated and the curtains trembled like when my dad's truck used to pull up to the driveway at midnight. But he wasn't ever coming home. Bruno flung open my door and scooped me out of bed. We stumbled toward the bright hall light like moths and huddled in my doorway. The rolling of the ground felt like wild animals at our feet trying to carry us away. Across the hall, I watched my mom's face tighten and her arms stretch out to press her palms against her bedroom's doorframe as if she were holding the house together. We heard shattering glass and heavy thuds. When the rolling stopped, we stayed still, only our eyes darted back and forth. Rain tapped against the window and the neighborhood German shepherds howled while we all held our breath. The house did one more shimmy and then settled for good.

"That was a four-point-five, four-point-seven max," Bruno said, finally relaxing his grip on my shoulders.

"That felt more like a six," my mom said.

"You're both wrong," I said as I made my way back into the room. "It was a seven-point-five."

"Careful, Violeta!" my mom shouted.

My twelve glass globes remained perfect and unbroken on top of my dresser. One for each sign of the zodiac. Instead of snow, gold glitter adorned the lion globe and tiny aqua diamond flecks swirled around the crab. Those were my star signs: Leo and Cancer. A predator and a disease. I shook them up, one in each hand, and watched the glitter fall around the red claws and roaring gold teeth.

The morning news lady said it was a four-point-five and reminded everyone to restock their emergency kits. Bruno pumped his fist in the air to celebrate winning a bet nobody made. "Told you! I've got an inner Richter scale."

The only casualty of the quake in our house was the mess of books on the living room floor and the shattered ceramic turtle-shaped toothbrush holder my mom had had since she was a teenager. She looked so sad when she swept it up but she doesn't cry anymore.

"I have to work late for a meeting tonight. Wait for your brother in the library so he can bring you home."

Bruno grumbled and capped his pen. He closed his sketchbook and zipped up his backpack. "I'm interviewing at the animal shelter right after school. Why can't she just take the bus?"

Mom pushed past me with the dustpan. "Your sister can't take the bus alone."

"I'm almost eleven," I said, as Bruno poured a glass of orange juice and handed it to me.

"I'll call Miss Rodriguez. She'll give you a ride." The broken turtle clinked into the trash can.

"Cindy hates me."

"Nobody hates you."

"Cindy hates me."

My mom shot me a look I'd only seen her give Bruno. I shut my eyes and drank my orange juice.

"You're going to get a ride with Miss Rodriguez."

Bruno exhaled so hard I could smell the garlic from last night's dinner from across the kitchen counter. "I'm ready to go now," he said. The keys jangled when he took them off their hook.

I pulled on my silver backpack and my mom nudged me toward the door. She had only one turquoise stud in. "Forgetting something?" I pointed to her naked ear.

"Every morning," she said with a sigh, tugging on her earlobe before opening the front door and handing me my blue chrome lunch box. "Here," she said. "Today is Wednesday. Cookie Day." She winked at me and even though I was mad at her for making me go home with Cindy, I didn't want her to be mad at me. Bruno honked the horn.

" 'Bye," I said, then kissed her on the cheek before pulling on my hood and running outside to the Roach. We called it that because it was dark copper, rode low to the ground, and just wouldn't die.

Bruno popped open the passenger door. "Seat belt's still busted. Gotta ride in the back."

I crawled to the backseat without putting up a fight. I loved riding in the backseat of the Roach. When it rained, it smelled like motor oil and leather, just like our dad.

* * *

The school's asphalt playground was covered in puddles. Our morning break was rained out and Miss Daria let me stay in the classroom to play with Oliver while the rest of the class went across the hall to the library. Oliver ate carrots from my hand and his white fur felt like a rich lady's coat. I loved his red eyes the most. Devil eyes, that's what Cindy called them. Whenever one of the boys took Oliver out of his cage, she'd squeal and refuse to feed him. She was the only person in the school who didn't like rabbits. She was the only person Oliver had ever bitten.

"Miss Daria? Do you think Oliver is scared of the dark?"

Miss Daria looked up from her desk and smiled. "What makes you think that?"

I shrugged. "He just looks like he's seen things, you know? He's here at night, when it's all dark and quiet. Like, he's always by himself."

"He's not by himself right now."

"But what about when I leave? When we all leave and he's here alone at night when it's dark. Isn't he scared?"

"Animals are guided by instinct. They know how to protect themselves. Oliver knows he has it good here. He knows we love him, and that gives him courage."

I'm not looking for comfort, I am asking questions because I want to know the answer. Are rabbits afraid of the dark? Do they get scared of sudden movements? How do I gain the trust of animals that are soft and small?

The sun peeked through the clouds at lunchtime. While everyone lined up to go to the cafeteria, I snuck away to eat my lunch on the bench of the Virgin Mary's grotto that was carved into rock on the side of the church. It was a hidden cave, my secret spot. Inside were all sorts of pretty flowers the nuns grew and a special area to light candles for prayer. The nuns didn't let students in the grotto without a teacher, but after my dad died, the nuns let me spend as much time as I wanted in there. When I got to the grotto gate, the iron door was locked and Sister Cathy stood there like a guard with her hands on her hips.

"I knew I'd find you here," she said. I gulped as she put her hands on my shoulders. "It's not safe in there, Violet. There's broken glass and rocks everywhere from the earthquake. We can't have you playing in there today."

I protested, but Sister Cathy swatted away my words. She pointed forward, straight in the direction of the school cafeteria.

I hovered near the door. The whole school had already found their seats and I would have to walk across the middle aisle to find my classroom's table. My heart was beating as fast as Marie's was right before it stopped forever. Because of Marie, Cindy called me Bird Girl, which wasn't so bad until it turned into Turd Girl. I imagined hearing the whispers in the cafeteria, chanting the nickname I didn't want.

"You okay, Violet?" Mr. Elliot asked. I was glad to see him. His tie was covered in alligators wearing top hats. "Are you buying lunch today or did you bring your own?"

I lifted my lunch box and hoped he would walk me over to Miss Daria and the fifth-grade table. Just then, Sister Rita rang the bell and cleared her throat. It was like someone hit the mute button on the entire room.

Mr. Elliot pointed to an empty seat at the end of the eighth-grade table in front of us. "You can sit here today, my permission. Hurry, before she starts," he whispered. Sister

Rita didn't have any patience because she hated children. My brother told me she once took away a kid's food because he sneezed during the sign of the cross.

"Let us pray." Sister Rita's high-pitched voice screeched across the room. Total silence. I bowed my head and looked around at the grown-up uniforms of the kids around me. White shirts and plaid skirts, no jumpers like mine.

"Hey," one of the boys whispered. "You're in Miss Daria's class, right?"

I didn't look up.

"She married?"

"Shh," said the girl next to him. "She's, like, thirty years old. Way too old for you."

"I don't care."

Amen. The magic word. The mute button clicked off and sound returned to the cafeteria.

I glanced up to see his face. Victor Fierro. I was sitting with Victor Fierro's crew. I heard Sarita gave herself a heart tattoo with a ballpoint pen and a needle. Carlos was once caught with a blade tucked inside the sole of his shoe. Victor had been caught with worse. They had bad reputations but their uniforms always had the most perfect pleats.

Victor stared at me and took a bite of his cold pizza. "You Bruno's little sister, right?" A piece of mashed ham flew out of his mouth when he spoke. "Too bad he fucked up his knee. Could've been the next Maradona."

"Mm-hm," I said.

"Aye. Is it true you ate a dead bird?" Victor asked.

Sarita burst out laughing.

Victor laughed. "What?" he said, and lifted his shoulders in an exaggerated shrug. "I'm just asking."

"No," I said. I'd answered this question before. "I gave her CPR."

Sarita laughed harder. "CPR? That shit doesn't work on birds."

"It doesn't always work on people," Carlos mumbled.

Victor leaned over the table, closer to me. "What you got in there?"

I kept my lunch box closed. I didn't want to eat in front of them.

"I said, what you got in your box?"

I traced a star on the table with my index finger and looked down. I traced another one on top of the first one, then one more. They all watched me. I felt their eyes on my hands.

"Leave her alone, dude. Es una tontita," Sarita said, while tapping the front of her head.

Star after star after star.

"You ask Karen to the dance yet?" Carlos asked Victor, distracting him.

Victor mumbled.

"Weak," Sarita said.

Victor turned his attention away from me. I was invisible again. My stars always worked, they always protected me. I opened up my lunch box and the leftover eggplant looked good, but it was too messy to eat and the cheese smelled like feet. I took out my cookies and closed the box back up. They smelled like warm butter and cinnamon. My stomach growled.

"Cookies!" Victor shouted.

Bruno told me it was easy to make friends. All I had to do was smile and share. If I shared my favorite cookies with Victor's crew, then I would only have one left over for me, but maybe I would have three new friends. "Do you want one?" I opened up the plastic bag of my mom's special-recipe chocolate chip cookies and moved them to the middle of the table.

Victor shoved his greasy pizza hands in the bag and popped a whole cookie in his mouth like a piece of popcorn. Sarita took one out and sniffed it. Carlos ignored me. I reached for the last two cookies, I couldn't wait to eat them. As soon as I opened my mouth to take a bite, Victor spit out a soppy wet wad and made a barfing sound.

"Gross!" Sarita said. She pushed herself away from the table, dropping her cookie on the floor. Everyone at the table stopped talking and stared at us.

"What is this shit?" Victor shouted. He pulled up his shirt and wiped his tongue.

"They're zucchini chocolate chip. My mom made them for me."

"Zucchini? That's not cookie food, what kind of stupid bitch puts vegetables in—"

Before he could finish, I swung my lunch box across his face. By the time Sister Rita reached us, Victor was on the floor and his cheek was streaked with blood.

My mom's parked car was a backslash between the two painted lines on the asphalt playground. I sat in the passenger seat, waiting for her to finish up with Sister Rita. She was taking a long time. I crawled in the back and stretched across the soft gray seats. Some of Victor's blood was still on my lunch box from where I busted open his nose. I really hoped he was okay. I sang, Sana sana, while rubbing my nose and pretending it was his. *Sana sana colita de rana, sana sana colita de rana*, over and over again.

My mom was angry at me and also angry she couldn't stay at home to yell about how angry she was at me.

"I was only defending you," I said.

"I don't need you to defend me. I need you to behave." She said it was the absolute worst day for me to act out. She didn't kiss me when she left the house to go back to the office. She ordered me to stay in my room. I wanted to obey her. Then I saw a bone in our rose garden. The earthquake must've brought it up.

* * *

Every Easter, we cut crosses out of construction paper during art class to decorate the auditorium for the exact same play the eighth-graders put on every year. Everyone wants to play Mary, Mother of God, no one wants to play Mary Magdalene. Everyone always claps at the end when zombie Jesus rises from his rocky grave. No one clapped for me when I tried to breathe life back into Marie.

Marie was the reason I stayed alone at school. Last year, I found her stuck in a wad of gum in a grassy patch next to the water fountain. She was a Costa's hummingbird, green and insect-like. I didn't notice her at first and almost stepped on her. When I saw she was in trouble, I tried to pick apart the sticky gum from her legs and the edges of her wings. I was very careful. I didn't want to tear her feathers or do anything that might hurt her. Her heart beat so fast that her little feathered body buzzed in my hands. My classmates crowded around and tried to take Marie from me and yelled at me to let her go, which terrified her. She died of fright, my mom said. Too much for her little body to take on.

Song for Marie
Little wing, you are a little wing
I have enough life for the both of us
Give me a feather, I'll give you breath
Little wing, I am here to be your little wing.

* * *

My curly hair collected beads of drizzle and the back of my neck started to itch when I stepped outside to investigate the bone. My pink rain boots squeaked and smelled like plastic. A tower of wild red roses grew up against our white cinder-block fence. Sometimes the flowers unfurled through the rusted cracks of my dad's toolshed and made a thorny nest against the ceiling. I opened the door to the shed and took in a deep breath of the dripping oil and metal. I poked around through the clutter of tools and discarded electronics for a shovel, finding only a hammer with a curved forked tongue and a thick metal ruler. I inhaled once more and marched back into the sloshy garden. The ruler was the perfect tool to lift the bone from the earth. I dug at the dirt around the bone with my hands and discovered its brothers and sisters. Sharp bones that looked like long teeth, fat and thick dirt-caked bones that felt like tree roots. I pulled out the spine and laid it on the grass. I knew it was the spine because it reminded me of a xylophone. I tapped my dad's ruler against the vertebrae but it didn't make music. More digging. Skinny bones and bones that looked like bat wings frozen in flight. I fanned them out against the spine and made rows of bones that looked like giant macaroni and rows out of the tiny bones that looked like bird beaks. The largest bone was buried deep, round and smooth, with curves and pockets. I used both hands to tug it out, smelling filthy pennies and wet rock the farther down I dug. The tarry earth sucked it back in, not letting go. I hooked my fingers into the sockets and pulled and pulled. The dirt finally let go with a squishy slurp and I fell backward onto the slick grass with the final, most important piece in my hands. The skull! A heavy animal head with two ivory daggers. I held the skull in front of my face like a mask. I tilted my face to the sky and sliced the air with its sharp fangs, pretending I could gut the clouds. I placed the head at the top of the spine and added the other bones like a puzzle. When it was all done and the shape of a wildcat became clear, I sprinkled red rose petals over my discovery. The petals clung. I sang a song like I had for Marie. When nothing happened, I pricked my finger with a rose thorn and made a new resurrection song. I sang and the ground rumbled.

Resurrection Song
Red rose petals
Silver straight edge

Rain like a slobbering beast
I need a time machine to see where you've been, you
need a kaleidoscope to see me
Mastodon, mastodon / That's not who you are
Promise: You'll never leave.
I'll keep you warm.
Give you a home, let you run free.
Mastodon, mastodon / That's not who you are
Take my hand—your saber-tooth
needs to be fed.
Promise: I'll share with you my flesh.

I named him Saturn because of the wide rings of his ribs.
When I gave him what he asked for, he swung his massive
head against me and pushed me into the ditch that once
housed his bones. In the mud and silt, I didn't feel any pain.
I remember that. I remember the dirt was warm and I was
cocooned. There was space for me to breathe. I heard the
earth's heartbeat, *thoom thoom*, pulsing heat and mineral-rich
tar. Did you know the earth holds its muscles in excruciating
stillness for you? It does, and it asks for very little in return.

* * *

I stopped telling the story of Saturn almost as soon as I started.
Your arm got like that because of a fire, they corrected me. First
in a concerned tone, then annoyed. After a few months, I
learned to agree. Sure, I said. The fire. The fire from the day
I got sent home for making Victor Fierro's nose bleed. The

fire from the neighbor's constantly burning candles that the afternoon aftershock tipped over. It was those timid candle flames that snaked into our yard and knocked me into the viscous backyard sinkhole. It was the fire that left everything else untouched but scorched my entire right arm. I watched the news every night during my hospital stay: slaughtered horses in Topanga, missing cats and dead raccoons in Griffith Park. The encampment at the L.A. River. The evidence was there. *Disease*, they countered. *Sociopaths*, *Satanists*. Sabers, I insisted to my mom. It was my Saturn.

* * *

After my snow globe phase in middle school, I got really into collecting cats in junior high. We could never have pets because my mom was allergic, but Bruno and I loved animals, Bruno probably more than me because he spent all his extra time working at the animal hospital. Saturn didn't visit me and the only animal stories on the evening news were about heroic dogs and aggressive sea lions. Because Mom's allergies kept me and Bruno from bringing home strays, I settled for figurines. It wasn't just Hello Kitty, I collected Maneki-neko, porcelain cats, cat office supplies, cat postcards, vintage salt-and-pepper shakers. The closest I got to a saber-toothed tiger was a miniature Smilodon fatalis skull replica from the Natural History Museum. I hung it over my bed and slept well.

By the time I graduated from high school, I had two drawers full of gloves. I wore them every day, knowing that if my classmates saw my bare arm they would ask too many questions or be cruel or, worse, pity me. At first they made fun of me, but at least they didn't hide it. Everyone eventually just got used to it, a couple freshmen even copied me. I had every color and texture: velvet white, polyester lime-green, satin pale pink, gloves with scalloped edges, leather ones with rivets, antique ones with embroidered flowers. Most were opaque. All were opera-length. On graduation day, I wore the navy sequined pair that matched my rented gown. That summer, I alternated between cotton gloves in a cheery yellow gingham print and white ones with tiny cherries. In August, for my eighteenth birthday, I bought a vintage orange leather pair for two bucks at the downtown thrift store, which I was told were really worth a few hundred dollars. That was what Gabe said anyway. It wasn't the only thing he lied about.

I'd met Gabe at the thrift store run by the methadone recovery clinic. He usually hung around outside the donation center smoking cigarettes, processing the boxes of wrinkled clothes and outdated textbooks no one wanted anymore. I went there every Tuesday, Blue Sticker Special Days, and he'd always say hi and tell me if anything particularly interesting had arrived, like the wooden Siamese cat or the almost complete fairy-themed chess set. He once set aside a box of mittens for me. They only covered my hands but I appreciated the gesture and paid the fifty cents to take them home. The next time I went in, looking for vases to put the red roses that were blooming a riot in our backyard, Gabe said he wanted to spend more time with me.

I waited for a night that my mom would be at the casino with her sister and Bruno would be working the overnight shift at the animal hospital, and wrote my address on a shopping receipt for him.

Gabe showed up close to midnight with lavender crescents under his eyes. He wasn't interested in my gloves or my snow globes or my bottles of colored sand. He wasn't interested in me, either. Immediately after stepping inside my house, he pulled a serrated knife from his belt. "Don't move," he said, then yanked my grandmother's crochet throw from the couch and threw it over our flat-screen TV. I stood watching him unplug and untangle the mess of wires Bruno kept promising to clean up. While Gabe's arms were full, I bolted through the living room, past the kitchen, and straight out the back door. I locked myself in my dad's toolshed and hid behind a bookcase full of old paint cans. I clenched a rusty hammer in one hand and imagined how I would hit him sharp and quick on his temple in the fight that never came.

Gabe didn't follow me. I waited until my heart stopped slamming against my ears to crack open the toolshed's door. Searching for movement in the dark house, I remained frozen until the kitchen phone started to ring. Slowly, I stepped out of the shed and toward the back door. I took a deep breath and flipped on the kitchen light. I was alone. The front door was wide open and the TV was gone. Gabe also stole Bruno's laptop, the microwave, my mom's jewelry box, and the pair of orange gloves I'd bought myself for my birthday. I didn't tell my mom all of that when she called again in the morning.

The investigator assigned to my case wore a body-clenching peach tank top that made her look half-naked. Her voice sounded like it was wearing a mask and she only looked at her notebook, not into my eyes. She spoke to me loud and slow because of the shade and shape of my face. "How exactly did you meet this man?"

"Where were your parents?"

"I see."

Scribble scribble scribble.

I didn't want to keep answering her questions. After seven years of hiding, I rolled the glove off my skin to show her exactly why I opened my door to a creep I thought could love me.

"What happened to your arm?" she asked in her real voice.

* * *

My mom and I made peace a few months later, while we were watching the morning news on our new, smaller TV. The anchor said it happened before sunrise. Blood and tufts of his hair were found just outside a liquor store. His toothless girlfriend said it happened where he picked up his nightly lottery ticket, so it must have been planned, he must have been stalked. The store owner described it as "a mountain lion with big-ass teeth." I gasped and covered my mouth with my hand. *Saturn!* The lady continued reading the news: "Law enforcement officers confirm the remains belong to Gabriel Hill, a parolee convicted of multiple home invasions and assaults."

My mom looked at me with her eyebrows raised and her mouth half-open. She leaned back into the couch and stared at the ceiling, rubbing her temples with her knuckles. Without turning her head, she waved me over to her side. I curled up on the couch next to her. I didn't say I told you so, but I wanted to.

* * *

I live in a studio apartment in Koreatown, on Wilshire Boulevard right next door to the Wiltern. I am only a couple of miles from the La Brea Tar Pits, so breezes on hundred-degree days smell like burned asphalt and kimchi. On concert nights, which is almost every night, people sing and clap as they walk back to their cars after a show. I don't know what offends me more, their terrible voices or their joy. I turn up my sound machine and trace stars on the wall with my finger. Star after star after star. When the edge of my window rattles, I freeze. It continues to tremble. I slide off the bed and lie flat against the floor. Barely a three-pointer.

My mom still calls after every earthquake. The Big One feels more and more like an unfulfilled promise instead of a warning but still, we keep our emergency kits stocked and our exit paths clear. When she's assured I'm fine, she wishes me a good night and I promise to visit her soon. I make a bed underneath the kitchen table to feel covered and protected. It's soft and comfortable and I fall back asleep.

Later that night, I'm jolted awake by a series of clangs outside my window. This is not an aftershock. A pregnant opossum has been hanging around the trash cans, I doubt she can make that much noise by herself. *Clang, clang.* I force myself up from my makeshift den and pull back the curtain to peer out the window. Between midnight and dawn, the hour of the blue sun. I squint to see if the opossum has finally given birth and that's when I see him. He is crumpled and heaving against the dumpsters. His tawny fur is covered with lacy patterns of dirt and grime. He looks up at me and there is a slickness of sick around his eyes. He dips his head and his sabers jam the metal trash can. *Clang.* This is not how I imagined him.

I race downstairs to meet my tiger. Little pieces of gravel and broken plastic pierce my feet. He sniffs the air as I approach and he rises slowly to greet me. I don't dare touch him but I know he needs me. I wave him toward me, and he follows. The iron gate of my apartment complex creaks as I usher Saturn into the courtyard. In the security lights, I can see the bones beneath his coarse coat so clearly. They appear then disappear under his fur as he slowly climbs the stairs to my apartment.

He falls asleep on the bed of blankets underneath my kitchen table. In my mind, he had a shimmering bronze and copper coat like his family of beautiful spotted warriors. He has returned to me ill and injured. The gash on his right thigh is surrounded by clumps of dried blood. His claws are splintered and the pads of his paws are worn from broken beer bottles and hot asphalt. One ivory fang is shorter than the other and sickly yellow buds sprout from his nose. Time hadn't played a role in my visions of him.

* * *

Bruno arrived just after sunset the next day. I heard him complaining about parking all the way up the stairs. I moved the iron pan I was using as a water dish and covered Saturn with a thin bedsheet—Bruno might freak out and I didn't know what my tiger would do if frightened.

"What's going on?" Bruno threw his keys and vet badge on the counter. He wore a gray sweatshirt over his polka-dotted scrubs. His thinning bleached hair and stretched earlobes made him look like an aging raver.

I pulled my fingers to my lips and hushed him. I pointed to the lump on the kitchen floor. "Don't make any sudden movements, okay?"

Bruno's eyes widened. "Is that a dead body?"

"Not yet." I lifted the sheet and watched my brother. His jaw dropped and he covered his mouth. Saturn's eyes fluttered but he remained still.

Bruno swayed. He lowered himself to the floor and knelt before my tiger. He pulled his hands out of his sweatshirt and spread them open, palms up, at his side. He looked like he was asking for forgiveness, an old Catholic school habit. I knelt next to him and placed my burned palm over his.

The next day, Bruno brought antibiotics. Saturn ignored the hamburger meat I left on his dinner plate. He did drink half a cup of water, which Bruno said was a good sign, even though he remained immobile. In my mid-twenties, I went through a tea towel and tablecloth phase; I had enough linens to keep Saturn's bed fresh for months if his recovery demanded more time. Bruno checked my tiger's heartbeat and carefully, very carefully, looked into his mouth. "He isn't in pain," he said. "But he will be. We can make it easier for him."

We. Now Saturn was ours.

I cracked the window and turned on the fan to keep my apartment from smelling like a kennel. For days, Saturn barely moved. Bruno cleaned his wounds and we slipped painkiller and antibiotics into pieces of cheese and sliced ham. Bruno then taught me how to inject the medicine into Saturn's bloodstream. Instead of getting better, Saturn began to breathe heavily, then go through long periods where it was like he wasn't breathing at all. Bruno and I took turns watching him at night. "What are you going to do with him if he gets better?"

I couldn't answer.

"You need to think about that, Violeta. He isn't a pet."

Soon, Saturn stopped eating and would only drink water if I wrung a soaked towel over his mouth. Bruno left a cocktail of fatal pills on the counter. "Don't be selfish. He'll feel like he's falling asleep."

* * *

Song for Saturn
You made your promise true
Your claws crave the sink of earth.
Your family waits for you on the other side
So does mine.

I hum as I wipe Saturn's face with a warm washcloth. I am making a mess on my kitchen floor. He opens his eyes and watches me. I show him my arm. He licks it. The stinging heat of his tongue burns off eighteen years of numbness.

* * *

This is how it happened: The skeleton collected itself into a terrible form. The red rose petals stretched into sinewy nerves and connected the thin slivers of toes and tarsals to lumpy hunks of joints. The mass of dirty bones and red petals lifted the fanged skull. The head remained steady despite the delicate disks and twigs responsible for supporting its massive weight. He asked for my help by opening and closing his jaw, slow and humble. I said yes and fed my arm to Saturn. My arm went as far as it could and his sabers rested against my heart. My knuckles grazed the underside of his vertebrae. Inside the belly of a million years, you will find magma, not ice.

* * *

"You were always close, weren't you?" I smooth the brush across Saturn's pelt and thank him for taking care of me. I take out my memory box and show him drawings I made of him when I was in school and a collection of his stories I clipped from the paper. When I show him pictures of my mom and dad, I think I hear him purr.

Saturn stretches his clawed paws and yawns. The inside of his mouth is filled with scaly white splotches. The gash on his thigh is shrinking yet not completely healed. He drinks water from the iron pan and juts his dry nose in the air. I have made him a good meal. Rare steak, tuna salad, chicken tenders, and mashed potatoes. When Saturn finishes his dinner, I open the front door to let in a fresh breeze. The boom and shrieks of next door's concert force their way into my apartment. My tiger sniffs the air and his eyes dilate. The sides of his body puff in and out as he inhales rapid streams of air. He smells something he wants.

Strengthened by the water and rich meat, he rises. I step back and watch him wobble to his feet. One paw in front of the other, his shoulder blades fold in and out like the gears of a machine as he makes his way outside. Saturn walks to the edge of the staircase and dips his paw down to the first step as if testing a pool of water. He jerks his paw back and settles onto his haunches. I shut the apartment door and press the button for the elevator.

Saturn limps steadily out of the elevator and across the courtyard to the gate. He presses his nose against the curly-cued iron and lets out a low growl. I obey. The gate screeches open to Wilshire Boulevard.

The night is lit by strobing electronic billboards. Saturn was never far from me and he is accustomed to the lights and the noise. We walk together. His nose in the air and strings of drool dangling from his open mouth. He is following a scent. The bodies around us press themselves against the buildings. Fingers point, hands cover their mouths. Saturn's limp corrects itself and soon we are making the world turn with the movement of our feet. Saturn and I, we control gravity and time. High-pitched shrieks go off like alarms as we pass. Cars slam to a stop and I hear metal and glass clash and shatter. The bubbling tar pits are close. I smell the thick asphalt that entices my

Saturn and I don't notice the moment when his gravity breaks free from mine. He is bounding down the sidewalk. I race to catch up and push through the soft bodies wrapped in denim and leather. I knock someone to the ground. They yell and throw a cup of half-eaten frozen yogurt at me. They can't stop me but the cars can. I run across the street with my eyes closed hoping they will slam on their brakes at the sight of me and when they don't and their horns blare and I fall in the middle of the road, Saturn roars, ROARS, and the city stops. He prods me up from the street with his commanding fangs and I see the drivers' faces full of wonder and horror. An electric joy bolts through my limbs and I rise and sprint and Saturn and I, we race down Wilshire together. I am laughing and I am singing. I leap when he leaps, I scramble over the hoods of cars he has trampled. His roar is the song I didn't know I could sing.

We arrive at the gated park and leap over the gold saber-toothed tiger at the entrance to the La Brea Tar Pits. I follow him to the edge of the prehistoric black lake where the fiberglass mammoth is eternally sinking. A helicopter circles overhead. Its spotlight skates across the tar, looking like a comet trapped underneath the earth, sending up desperate beams of light. I stroke my tiger and kiss the space between his ears. My tiger, my Saturn. I wrap my arms around him and command every part of myself to record him: the coarseness of his fur against my skin, the heat of his breath on my neck, the milkiness of his eyes, his immortal smell of leather in the rain. Stroking his soft ear with my burned fingers, I hum: *Mastodon, mastodon / That's not who you are.* I hold on until he is back in the earth, I hold on to him everywhere I go.

CARLOS
ACROSS SPACE
AND TIME

Ruby, angled black bob with wisps of stubborn hair tucked behind her ears and bright fuchsia lip gloss staining her lips, pulls the trigger of a fluorescent-yellow gun. Grapefruit-sized bubbles drift away from the Orb Wand's bulbous plastic barrel and float into the air. Across the tiled floors and surrounded by exhausted moms in Baby Phat jeans trying on Victoria's Secret lotions, an oversized supermodel in a pink satin bra challenges Ruby to a staring contest. Ruby hasn't won once, not even close, during the past four months hyping pan-flute CDs and overpriced geodes in the mall. Adriana Lima's green eyes, smoldering under smoky black shadow, taunt Ruby throughout her shift. *You'll never have me, you'll never be me.*

"Ruby? Is that you?" A woman in a white V-neck tank top interrupts Ruby's trance, forcing her to focus on the familiar but unplaceable face in front of her. Ruby's attention is drawn down to the little hands tugging at the bottom seam of the woman's shirt. They belong to a boy who is wrapped around her knee like a sloth on a tree. His round brown eyes are lined in thick black lashes. He watches the bubbles drift away from the bubble gun and over his head.

"It's me. Lissette. Lissette Martinez."

Ruby looks up and sees a face of the past superimpose itself onto the one in front of her. "Liz? I didn't recognize you."

Liz laughs. "Yeah, I had a kid and finally got boobs and an ass."

"Your face is fatter, too."

Liz's smile flattens. "Yeah. That, too." She strokes the little boy's hair. "This is Roque. Roque, say hi to Ruby. She's an old high school friend."

Ruby raises her eyebrow. Friend is too generous but how do you explain *this is the girl I let copy my algebra homework* to a kid? Ruby smiles and leans forward. She asks in a voice much lighter and higher than her own, "How old are you?" and the kid buries his face in his mom's jeans. Ruby looks up at Liz for an answer.

"He eats with utensils. We talk about birds and cats. He picks out his own clothes."

"So, like, two and a half or something?"

Liz shrugs, "Sure, if you're counting that way."

How else you gonna count? Ruby thinks. *Cut him open like a tree?*

Roque reaches out and grabs the toy. Liz is quick and snatches the gun from his hands, holding it up to her bare shoulder. "He's kinda careless. I don't want him to break it."

"It's fine. They got a ton of them in the back." Ruby points to the empty store. "Not like we're going to run out anytime soon."

Liz frowns, but relents. Roque pulls the trigger and his bright giggle accompanies the mechanized whir of the Orb Wand's inner fan. She scoots her son away from the main entrance and toward the Wishing Well of Healing Stones, a wide and shallow dish of polished rocks. Liz picks up a smooth black stone and brings it close to her face, studying it. "What do you know about obsidian?"

"It's black. Shiny." Ruby sticks her hand in the cool rocks and pulls out a smooth black sphere. She closes one eye and looks at herself in the stone's reflection. Her hair is longer and darker than it was in high school and she is surprised Liz recognized her, only because Ruby doesn't remember much about anything. Because she dropped out at the end of junior year and went through a brief but intense magic mushroom phase, the only reliable memories Ruby has of her classmates are trapped in a thick green yearbook with a gold *1999* in Old English font stamped on the cover, lost somewhere on her closet floor. What Ruby now remembers about Liz is that she didn't eat meat and the boys were crazy for her. One specifically. "Hey, you still keep in touch with your ex?"

"Cuál ex?"

"Your ex Carlos. Carlos Flores with the big ears."

Ruby barely hears when Liz says, "Carlitos is dead."

In a flash, she sees his face and smells his cologne, hears his raspy voice talking shit on their fourth-period history teacher. One of Roque's bubbles floats into the well of stones and pops. "Carlos? Carlos Flores?" Ruby says his whole name, giving Liz a chance to correct herself. "Sonia's little brother? That Carlos?"

"Yes. That Carlos. My Carlos. Right after graduation." Liz narrows her eyes. Now it's her turn to inspect every inch of Ruby, up and down. "I didn't know you knew him."

Ruby opens her mouth to explain she didn't *know* him

know him, but it doesn't matter. Carlos is dead and her mouth is so dry. "What happened?"

Liz drops her voice to a whisper. "Graduation party." The muscles in her face twitch. She's clenching her jaw or biting her cheek. Ruby leans in closer. "He went out to his car to smoke or something. Just sitting in the driver's seat and some guy walks up to him." Liz glances at Roque and then discreetly puts a finger to her head, pointing the barrel of her finger to her temple.

Nothing to say, Ruby puts her hand to her mouth.

"Did they get who did it?"

"Cops only care that the body count is high." Her voice trailed off. "But yeah. It got taken care of." Liz tosses the black stone back into the well. "Why is it always a gun?" she says. They watch Roque making bubbles. He laughs when they pop against the floor, leaving a faint wet semicircle on the speckled carpet. Liz looks Ruby in the eye and repeats, "I didn't know you knew him."

The whirr suddenly stops and the toy dribbles out the last bit of soap. Roque's face falls.

"Shoot. It needs more batteries. I'll be right back."

"Don't. I'm not going to buy it for him." In one quick motion, Liz takes the toy from Roque and hands it to Ruby, then scoops him up in her arms and heads for the door. "Sorry," she says on her way out. "This is going to get loud." She waves goodbye and the kid's wails and screeches echo throughout the mall until they reach the escalator.

Adriana Lima's eyes take on a menacing glare. Ruby hadn't thought of Carlos for years. Now she sees his face in each guy that walks by. She points the Orb Wand at them and pulls the trigger. They fall to the ground and a pool of burgundy blood oozes out of them. How far would news of their death ripple out? There is this pressure against her eyes like she wants to cry. *What right do I have to mourn him?* When she gets home, she digs around the hallway closet for her mom's old Singer. Jagged line after jagged line, Ruby teaches herself how to sew.

Marvelous Earth employees typically do merchandise maintenance after hours or before their shift, and never on the counter behind the cash register. But the mall is dead and her stoned coworker is sitting in front of the display TV watching a whale documentary, so Ruby decides to pass the next couple hours squirting ketchup onto a rag and polishing the store's copper wind chime. A mindless and satisfying activity. She doesn't notice Liz until she's standing in front of the register.

"He still crying about the Orb Wand?"

Liz sets a handful of obsidian rocks on the counter. "He loved that thing."

Ruby tosses the rag in the trash and wipes her hand on her work apron. "I have an employee discount if you want to get it for him."

"No. I mean. Thanks. I don't like him playing with guns."

Ruby rings up the obsidian and places them in a black velvet bag. She feels a twinge of benevolent power after punching in her employee discount code for the first time.

Liz carefully tucks the bag in her purse. "When are you off?"

"I can take my break anytime."

"No. Not here. I mean. You should come over. We've been staying with my mom since Roque's dad's been deployed." She leans in closer and drops her voice to a whisper. "I need to talk to you about Carlos."

The next day, Ruby parks on the street and walks up the two flights of stairs to Apartment H. Liz opens the door and Ruby is greeted by braying sound effects and dramatic proclamations of a TV psychic. "Roque's with my mom at the park. I gotta go to class in two hours." Liz looks annoyed as she waves Ruby inside, as if all this weren't her idea in the first place.

Down the narrow hallway, Liz opens the door to her bedroom. It looks like how it probably did in high school, pale pink walls and a vanity crowded with photos. A faded 2Pac poster taped next to a white bookshelf filled with Roque's toys and puzzles. She opens another door to the attached bathroom and motions Ruby to follow her in.

The wall above the sink is covered with a thick black cloth. The rectangle vanity is crowded with cans of mousse and tubes of mascara. Ruby recognizes the bag of rocks from Marvelous Earth scattered around the beauty supplies, and right next to a bottle of hot-pink nail polish, a hammer with a worn wooden handle. Liz closes the door and runs her hand over the light switch. The sunlight through the small window above the toilet keeps the room illuminated. "I have to show you something." Liz pulls down the black cloth to reveal the bathroom mirror, broken and shattered into sharp cracks and triangles. Surprised, Ruby steps back, then leans in closer. Squinting, she sees shiny obsidian embedded in the empty spaces between the mirror fragments.

"What is this?"

Liz takes the black fabric and stands up on the toilet lid to hook it onto two nails above the window. Darkness. As Ruby's eyes adjust, she sees flashing blue currents of light between the stones and broken glass, pulsing through the mirror like veins.

"Liz. What *is* this?"

Liz flicks on a lighter and lights a small white votive. She grabs Ruby's hand and pulls her in closer so her stomach presses against the edge of the countertop. "Do you remember Bloody Mary?"

Ruby gulps, her throat is so dry. "Is that what we're doing here?"

"Not exactly. You can't see the future in this mirror. You see other versions of life."

Ruby tries to wriggle her hand free. Liz's acrylics dig in like a bear trap. "Don't be afraid. It's like being in a movie and watching it at the same time." With her free hand, Liz points to their reflections. Their two disembodied glowing heads float in the violet black background, bolts of electric blue light snaking through the mirror cracks.

"Whatever you do," Liz whispers, "don't look away until you're all the way inside. I'll be here when you come back."

Hypnotized, Ruby watches her face warp into a swirling whirlpool of eyes, lips. It splits and duplicates and now there are many Rubys where there had only been one.

She hears the crack of glass and she is now on the other side, staring back at herself. Her body is wrapped in a flowy yellow dress she would never wear and her arms are covered in rose and orchid tattoos. Ruby's head is full of someone else's memories and she now is a passenger in another version of her life.

Ruby in the Second World

Ruby clears her throat and reads the words from an open book:

> Carlos kicks it with the party crew girls. My best friend calls them the chachias. Two clicks down from cholas, the chachias cloak themselves in Lycra and polyester and clack their French tips against the metal trough sink in the girls' bathroom. They stand in front of the foggy and scratched chrome stick-on mirrors and, with their steady hands, pierce safety pins through their eyelashes to comb out clumps of dried mascara. Mirrors, like colored shoelaces and sports logos, invoke trouble and are forbidden at our school. I push my way through the chachias clustered at the trough and pump out a puff of powdered soap . . .

Ruby finishes her reading and smiles at the applause. She welcomes the audience questions and deploys her rehearsed responses and origin story: "I started writing during my junior year in high school, fourth period creative writing class. It really saved my life.

"Just random ideas that come to me, come *through* me,

when I least expect it. It's like I'm channeling something else, you know?

"Literature major, then immediately got my MFA. Worried that if I took a break from school I'd have to get a real job lolol."

A woman in the front row wearing a burgundy bandage dress and oversized sunglasses stands up and announces her question. "That guy you kill off in the first chapter, Carlos. How did you know how to write him?"

The fuck? Ruby's face spasms. "Spoiler alert," Ruby says, trying to laugh it off.

"No. I mean," the woman continues, "did you know Carlos? Like in real life."

The audience looks expectant, not annoyed. They want Ruby to answer, to prove how down she is, to prove that she knew a guy who got shot, that gang war raged in her neighborhood just like the newspapers claimed. They want her to be who they expect her to be. She is and she isn't. She is both a caricature and an aberration, with an immeasurable range of Rubys in between. "The character is a composite," she finally says. "All of them are. Different names, different faces. I know there is someone mourning a Carlos who was killed by a gun. I've mourned someone killed by a gun. So have many of you. Those stories don't always make the news. So yes, Carlos is based on someone I knew. But no, I didn't know Carlos."

A few people in the audience snap their fingers in approval and Primary World Ruby bites the inside of her cheek to keep from screaming, *Where the fuck am I?*

The lady in the burgundy dress is first in line to have her book signed. Ruby gives a quick forced smile and glances down, opening the book to the title page. "Who should I make it out to?"

"Doesn't matter." The woman takes off her glasses and leans forward. "None of this matters." Ruby drops the pen and looks into the woman's eyes, recognizing her now as a Liz.

"What am I supposed to be doing here?"

She taps on the book. "This was your chance, Ruby. All these people, now each time they read about him, he dies all over again. Alone."

"Is that what you see in the future?"

Liz rolls her eyes and puts her sunglasses back on. "It's not time travel, pendeja. You should've written him a better death. We still need to find him a better death."

Ruby in the Primary World

Ruby gulps down the strawberry soda. Liz's mom's kitchen is covered in colorful chickens: fancy hens on the curtains, proud roosters on her sandwich plate. Little eggs on the drinking glass. Liz refills her glass, telling her the sugar will help with the shock.

"Carlos gave me a pair of diamond earrings at the end of junior year, trying to get me back. I thought they were fakes and never wore them. Until the funeral." Liz paused to clear her throat.

Ruby's eyes sting.

"After all the crying, I just got really mad. Like, enraged. Why him, you know? Why any of them? I lost it and started pulling all my shit out of the closet, throwing shoes across the room. And then I saw myself in that mirror and just got so mad at myself for not staying with him, thinking maybe. Maybe." Liz's jaw tightens. "I yanked off the earrings and threw them at the mirror."

"Earrings did that? No way. That thing is in like a million pieces."

"Forty-thousand seventy two. So far. Each time I go in, the glass splits at least ten more times. The obsidian keeps it from crashing down but I have a really curious kid. I'm terrified he's going to figure out how to use it someday and accidentally find a world where he's in Iraq instead of his dad or I'm a serial killer. I'm going to mess up my kid and it's not even going to really be me."

Ruby closes her eyes and cracks her neck. "Just get rid of it, Liz. My cousin knows a guy. He'll take the whole mirror straight off the wall and put in a new one. Detail your car, too." She opens her eyes. Liz's stare is wide and desperate.

"I can't. Not until we observe a better death."

"We? What's this have to do with me?"

Liz knots her fingers together and says with impatience at the edge of her voice, "Estamos enredados. He's a part of you, too. If he means something to one of us, he should mean something to all of us."

Ruby rubs her forehead, trying to help her brain catch up.

"All I'm asking you to do is look in the mirror and tell me what you see. If you observe it, then it becomes real."

"What if I don't want to?"

"You will. You always do."

Ruby in the Third World

On graduation night, after the student model ungracefully clomps down the auditorium runway in Ruby's striped black-and-white satin gown, after her best friend Casey jubilantly accepts the student designer of the year award, after the tears and the proud parents, Ruby celebrates by sprawling out in Casey's backyard with a stolen bottle of champagne.

"Here's to Mr. Young, for making us design ugly-ass dresses no one will ever wear." *Clink.*

"Here's to Alexander McQueen, for always showing us the way." *Clink.*

"Here's to Ms. Sledge, my junior year fourth-period sewing instructor, who pulled every silk string to get me into this *fucking insane* fartsy high school for senior year." *Clink.*

"To Hien and his bomb-ass chronic." *Clink, clink.*

Ruby breathes deep and reaches her hand out to the blurry stars and skinny crescent moon. The sun is rising in London. "Are you going to miss me?"

"I don't even want to think about it. One more month."

"One more month," she repeats. "Then I'll be deep in the land of Moz and Westwood, saying shit like, *Cheers!* and *Let's go shark birds.*"

"What the fuck is sharking birds?"

Ruby tries to get one more drop out of the empty bottle. "Something I've always wanted to do."

Two miles east, Carlos is dead in the driver's seat of his car. His death, and his life, mean nothing to her.

Carlos in the Two Hundred and Forty-Fourth World

The fashion vocabulary Carlos began building in his junior year fourth-period sewing class proved to be a valuable foundation for his first year abroad. By the end of autumn, he was dropping new phrases (Madame Grès pleats, Schiaparelli pink, innit, bruv) in the California lilt that had initially confused his classmates. And now, just before the end of the school year, while their classmates struggle with their spring project, he and his flat mate/design partner Nalin have just signed a contract with Comme des Garçons and are throwing a rave in their cavernous new loft to celebrate.

Carlos watches everyone he knows and wants to know dancing and glittering in his new loft. Jungle beats snake through the crowd and Nalin dances next to his DJ girlfriend like he has elastic bones. Carlos makes his way toward them. In his hands, a ridiculous gold gun he bought as a joke from a sidewalk vendor around Tower Bridge. It will live in their new workspace, a cheeky keepsake of their unexpected success, a talisman to remind them of the Cali gangsta and London lanksta lifestyle everyone assumed they had.

Carlos steps behind the DJ and taps Nalin on the shoulder. Everyone can see them. The reporters from the dailies lift their recorders and cameras. The models who are all taller than him raise their glasses. Carlos smiles and pulls the gun from his waistband. He points the barrel at his own face to kiss it before dramatically handing it off to his truest friend. It's just supposed to look good for the pictures. The screams are deep and sorrowful. Again, Carlos's life ends with a hole in his head.

Across the pond, in her sophomore community college sewing class, Ruby of the Two Hundred and Forty-Fourth World reads in *Women's Wear Daily* a feature about the devastating promise of Carlos's work and his last days. Ruby traces her fingers over the picture of a hometown boy with dreams so much like her own. His Suavecito-perfected pompadour and close-cut sideburns hugging his baby face. And his designs! Her favorite is the bias-cut slip dress with dramatic bleeding heart appliqué and accessorized with a metallic red bandanna turban. *Very 2Pac meets Poiret,* says the caption, quoting a classmate. A denim micro dress with a mandarin collar featuring a six-inch Virgen de Guadalupe hand-embroidered over the heart. *Welcome to the Far East L.A.,* says the quote from his teacher. A one-piece white bathing suit with an exquisite Smile Now, Cry Later icon in black sequins stitched across the bust and torso. Ruby scoffs at the *For the theater lovers* caption.

The last lines of the obituary state that authorities found the vendor of the gold gun and arrested her for selling a deadly weapon. The poor old woman swears it was just a toy, a plastic nothing. She has no idea how the bullet got in there and neither does anyone else.

Carlos in the 10⁵ World

In this world, the atomic bomb goes off during fourth period. The ensuing tsunami claims Southern California for the ocean. All bodies and buildings sink to the floor, and salt-water-brined flesh is picked off by greedy lobsters and fish. A black-and-white-striped sea snake goes through Ruby's eye sockets and Carlos's shattered skull is home to a magenta starfish.

Carlos in the Primary World

Fourth-period history was in the bungalow all the way at the far end of the campus, close to the auto shop class, right up against the metal chain-link fence that separated the high school from the abandoned train tracks. Ruby slipped into her seat in front of Carlos. The school dress code was so strict that he made his own uniform: buzzed head, radiant white K-Swiss, baggy khakis that gathered and draped like a bustle around his skinny legs. That day, he switched out CK One for Gaultier's Le Male cologne. He sprawled across his desk using his gray hoodie like a pillow. *Another fight with his girl*, thought Ruby. Carlos lifted his head to acknowledge her. "I finally found your book."

"Did you bring it back?"

"I'm still looking at the pictures."

Mr. Palmer rolled out the television cart to the front of the classroom.

"Movie day," Carlos said. He tapped Ruby's shoulder with a pack of Starburst. "Don't take all the pink ones again."

Ruby picked out her favorites, leaving one pink square before handing it back. She opened her backpack and pulled out a Pepsi and placed it on Carlos's desk.

"School's almost over and he hasn't taught us shit. When do you think we're actually gonna learn something?" The soda hissed open.

Ruby shrugged. "Maybe after we graduate."

"Cleopatra had that special something," Mr. Palmer announced. "As you're going to see in this film, Cleopatra could make men do anything for her."

"Finally. Something related to actual history," Carlos muttered.

"You need to watch out for women who have *it*," Mr. Palmer continued. "Like, Karla, you got it. Jasmine, you have it, too." He went like that for the entire row of seats, his fifty-something-year-old eyes traveling down all the teen girls seated in front of Ruby. "Lisa's got it. Arlene's got it." Mr. Palmer looked straight at Ruby, then jumped to the row next to her. "You got it too, Flor. And be thankful that you do. You'll see that men will do anything for you. Even some women. Right, Ruby?"

A classroom full of heads turned to watch Ruby's reaction. She remained silent and still. Mr. Palmer switched on the TV and blithely moved on. Someone flicked off the lights and the opening music filled the room.

"Fuck that guy," Carlos whispered. "You're going to London, remember? You're gonna be a fashion designer, all fancy-

fancy." He nudged her shoulder and passed her the last pink Starburst. "This fucker will stay right here, eating cat food and hitting on kids."

That is the moment Ruby fell in love. Not as you fall in love with another person, but as you fall in love with a version of yourself described by a fortune-teller. *That curve of your heart line underneath your pinkie indicates a conflicted but weighty brilliance. Yes, you are the skeleton in black armor of the Death card, reaping a world of velvet and satin. One day hot pink fireworks will bloom in your sky, bright and eternal.* One day. That's right. You're right, Carlos. Fuck that guy, fuck this place.

Carlos in the Twenty-Sixth World

"Twenty bucks if you finish sewing my shorts?"

"Only if you wear them in public," Ruby shoots back.

Carlos holds up the black-and-white-striped fabric he picked out from Ms. Sledge's closet and laughs. "Never!"

A year later, Ruby attends his funeral. She wears his cologne and sobs quietly in the pew closest to the exit.

Carlos in the Seventy-Seventh World

In this world, Carlos's grandfather married a white woman, and so did Carlos's dad. This doesn't stop Carlos from digging up and exploiting José, his own undernourished inner Mexican. José is Carlos's buried first name and the only connection to his grandfather, a retired architect from Guadalajara. Unlike his grandfather, José Carlos doesn't speak Spanish or know the difference between chingada and chingadera, but he bolds the accent on José in all his emails as a warning to the recipient: *When you write me back, my name better look just like this.*

José Carlos debuts his new name in his book about walls and borders and Spanglish. He shaves off his light brown hair and grows out a cholo goatee for his author photo in preparation for his next appearance. His poems all include the greatest hits: "They still look at me funny," "They still look at me like I don't belong here," "They expect so little of me and look at me now." So fucked up, right? How *they* dominate the voices in your head so that even when you open your mouth to sing, it's really only about them. That is what the voices in Ruby's head say. The voices tell her to keep an eye on José Carlos, he is doing more damage than good. *Who are the voices, mijita?* her mom asks. *The ancestors*, she says.

José Carlos opens the night with the story that goes Books Saved My Life. It's his favorite for interviews and visits to schools where there aren't real mirrors in the bathrooms, only chrome stickers and powdered soap. But books don't save lives, just ask Primary World Carlos. If he could, Carlitos would tell you he had Ruby's *Lonely Planet London* in his hands at the exact moment the bullet went through his skull. He'd tell you he didn't know who shot him, he'd tell you that he didn't want to die. And, if the right people are attending the séance, Carlos will also admit he never read the guidebook but did keep it in the glove compartment to sort out the stems and seeds when rolling joints during work breaks. It was the book that saved his afterlife: he held it in his hands and saw the Tower Bridge in the final moment of his life. *I go back there every now and then*, he'd say, floating above our heads. *I like watching the snow. If I wasn't a ghost, I'd make little snowmen and shit. What do you mean, you haven't gone to London yet, Ruby? What the hell are you waiting for?*

Carlos in the Primary World

Ruby turns off her sewing machine and clips off the excess threads from her *Beetlejuice* costume. She promised Roque her costume wouldn't be a horror show, just scary enough so no one would steal his candy.

Before she heads out the door, Ruby digs out the yearbook from her closet. She finds him in the Flores row. She's seen him hundreds of times (she stopped counting after the Three Hundredth World), but there is no one like this Carlos. Peloncito, trying not to smile but dimples still peeking through. Carlos Flores's death happened in her solar system. He wasn't her sun or even an asteroid. He was more like a night of meteor showers witnessed only when the Santa Ana winds knocked out the power grid: an unexpected source of light in an uncertain time. Ruby tears out the photo and puts it in her pocket.

On her way to Liz's, she stops at the Dia de los Muertos festival downtown. The community altar still has room on the second-to-lowest tier. Ruby places his photo and a trial size of Le Male cologne next to a bouquet of magenta carnations. She knows she's not the only one who remembers him. She knows he doesn't need her to mourn him. He doesn't need you to mourn him. He needs us to remember his future in a different way.

Carlos in the Infinity

Carlos Flores sits at the kitchen table of his daughter's house. He wears his old khaki corduroys and a red flannel shirt. He checks his Lotto numbers and grumbles as he crumples up the orange ticket in his hand. His grandson's eighteenth birthday party will start in a few hours. He made fun of his daughter for hosting a party with a little cake and everything. "When I was eighteen, you know what I was doing?"

"Everything you shouldn't have been doing. That's why we're giving Miguelito a nice party. Now put up the streamers while I get ready."

Carlos rises from the table and stretches. He thinks he should have a big party for his ninetieth birthday. Malachi and Jacee are still hanging on and would be down for a real blowout. Carlos feels a cold lump in his throat and jiggles his Adam's apple. *That would be too much work*, he decides. *Have everyone drive out here for a big party, then drive back out a year or two later for my funeral. Too much hassle.* The cold lump is now lodged, blocking his breath. Carlos begins to cough, loud and deep. He leans on the table to brace himself and his coffee cup crashes on the tile floor.

His daughter runs into the room, hairbrush still in her hand. "Qué te pasa, Apá?"

But he doesn't answer. He pounds his chest, and finally he

coughs up the cold lump sitting in his throat, metal and small in his mouth. He spits it out and it clinks against the floor.

"Mira esto," he says, and picks it up. A flattened silver bullet.

"What the hell is that?"

"What the hell are you putting in your coffee?"

"This is serious. We need to go to the hospital."

He holds up the dime-shaped slug to the light and starts to hum a song from back in the day. *Dowop doo wah, do wop do wah ooh.* Carlos takes his daughter's hands and starts to dance, the bullet pressed against their palms. "I'm eighteen with a bullet."

He spins his daughter around and she looks at him como que se le botó la canica. He's a retired poet who survived an attempt on his life and an atomic bomb, of course he is used to that look, used to odd dreams and unexpected intrusions on his reality. These days he calms his mind with knitting and basic batik. His family knows this about him, knows when to just let him be. Carlos tilts his head so his daughter can choose whether to argue with a madman or let it go.

"If you cough up another one, I'm calling the ambulance."

That night he eats so much birthday cake and dances with his daughters and by himself. He flirts with his grandsons' girlfriends. He sings, he claps. He tells his family that he loves them and they pour him another shot.

When the party is over and the guests have gone home, Carlos takes a hot shower and carefully picks his last outfit of dark gray trousers, a bright yellow T-shirt from the last family reunion, and a cashmere navy sweater. He places the bullet on the nightstand and kisses the picture of his wife, promising to see her soon.

Carlos dreams he is walking across the Tower Bridge. He hears a liberating shatter of glass and feels an invigorating cold wind on his face. The faint figure of his woman approaches. Fiery meteors streak the sky and the snow cloaks him in a peaceful, endless night.

PAINT BY
NUMBERS

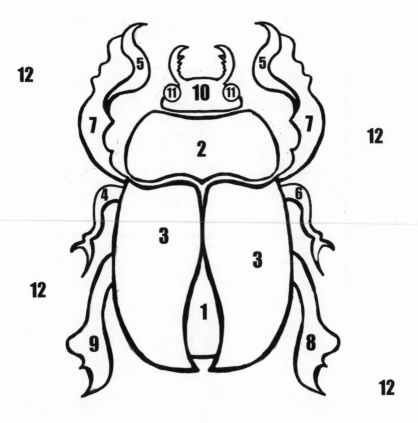

12

12

12

12

12

1 - The powdery **blue** of the blue death-feigning beetle. This desert-dwelling beetle secretes a wax that transforms its black skin for protection. The insect's matte ridged armor and an ability to play dead for hours ensure safety in a hostile environment.

2 - The deep navy **blue** uniform that is a cloak of impunity.

3 - The green-hued **blue** veins visible on the inner forearm, holding the gun steady. Practice makes perfect.

4 - **Blue**-violet of the bruise that forms around where the bullet enters the body.

5 - The electric **blue** of lights flashing in the police officer's living room while he scolds his teenage daughter about her obsession with DIY tattoo video tutorials.

6 - "**Blue** Mood" is the color of the lipstick worn by the officer's thirteen-year old daughter.

7 - The familiar deep navy-**blue** of the uniformed man knocking on the officer's door.

8 - The sky is a baby-**blue** over the head of the death-feigning man (_____). The death-feigning man wears a face that is not his own, in a borrowed body cloaked in the crisp uniform of impunity. He greets the man who took his life, who broke his son's heart, whose guilt was captured on video. He wraps his hands around the police officer's neck and, with the strength of two men, brings him to his knees. The daughter screams.

Do you see me? he asks. His skin contorts back to his true face, the one he had when he was alive. *Do you see me DO YOU SEE ME*

9 - The officer's icy **blue** eyes bulge and he pleads for his life.

The death-feigning man turns his head and demands an answer from the daughter, *DO YOU SEE ME*

Her blue lips part and she whimpers, "Yes."

He points to his own face. *SAY MY NAME*

"_____."

SAY MY NAME

"_____!"

He releases the officers's neck and as he gasps for air, the death-feigning man pulls out a

10 - black gun and shoots the officer twice in the head.

11 - The deep **red** spreads against the

12 - white tile.

MARIA,
MARIA

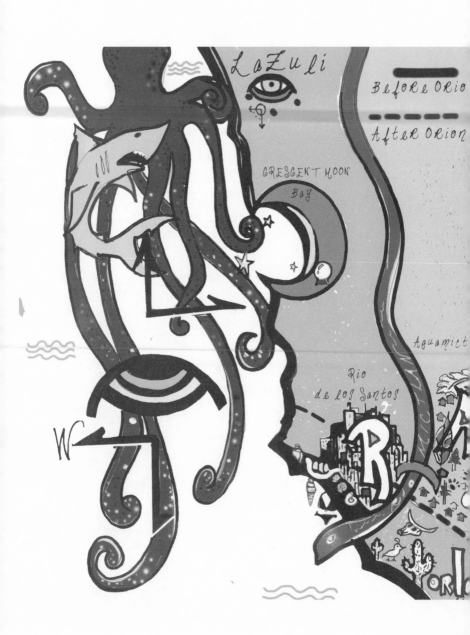

Maria Teresa Milfuegos, who prefers the name Maite, was born during the Orion Earthquake. The Big One. Her mother, Maria Lucia Milfuegos, spit out the sugarcane stick as the doula brought her daughter into the world, her screams as loud as the blaring tsunami siren. Sheltered from the falling buildings and fires of the terremoto's devastation, Maite grew up high in the hills of the gated coastal town of Crescent Moon Bay in a buttermilk-colored house shaped like a two-tiered wedding cake. Oval stained-glass windows adorned the rim of each tier like dots of icing. As the sun set, the light shone through the windows and bejeweled her and her mother's golden skin with reflected rainbow light. Only Maite had ever seen her mother this way, without the bobbed Cleopatra wig and sculptural gold earrings, without the mink eyelashes and layers of violet lipstick. Just Mom in a yellow sundress, coils of brown curls framing her bare face, teaching Maite how to prune the faded blooms of a rosebush. Mom with lemon verbena and rose hip tea before bed, singing along to Prince and Gal Costa. That was the memory that belonged only to her. All the other things, the velvet robes and gold-plated cobras— the patina of LaZuli—belonged to everyone else.

Even after she added the name "Mom" to her shifting identities, Maria Lucia's truest version of herself was LaZuli, the unexpected leader of millions desperate for otherworldly intervention in an uncertain society. Nouveau witches and street shamans adored LaZuli for her stylish séances and subversive astrological forecasts ("Libra: The scales of justice sometimes need to be tipped. Cancer: Use your ability to walk askew to infiltrate narrow, well-guarded crevices. Scorpio: There is power in numbers. Find your nest and sharpen your stinger.") For all of Maite's young life, she and her mother lived safe and secure off of LaZuli's product licensing, endorsements ("Cleanse your house of negative energy and grime with Fabuloso's Limpieza Total"), and select public appearances. LaZuli fully embraced the commercial attention of devotees who could afford her platinum bruja nameplate necklaces and $3,333-per-hour tarot card readings. At the time of her death, the celebrity psychic's best sellers were a Mayan Soul Cleanse vaginal bath and SMS protection spells for your smartphone.

Split yourself in half and send one part to an abandoned church on a Louisiana bayou and the other part to a twelve-year-old girl's bedroom in Northern California. The girl's bedroom walls are lilac and covered with posters of sharks and planets. The abandoned Louisiana church windows break from the water and wind rushing in. At the moment of her mother's death, Maite's knees buckled and her throat swelled. For an instant she was in the blue and green underwater with Maria Lucia, both their eyes wide and unblinking. Maite heard her mother's voice for the last time—declaring her love, dispensing a final and everlasting piece of esoteric wisdom, promising to come back—but she couldn't make out the words.

Maite, boxed in the lilac walls thousands of miles away from her mother, could only clutch her heart and weep. The evening news confirmed that on St. John's Eve, Hurricane Julia dragged LaZuli, and the two dozen devotees who refused to leave the side of their beloved psychic, to the bottom of Lake Pontchartrain. When reporting the tragic event, no newscaster in the country was fired for saying "Well, I guess she didn't see *that* coming."

A photographer had enticed LaZuli with the promise that she would be the first animated cover of *Hecate Couture*. It wasn't difficult to convince her, LaZuli couldn't refuse an opportunity to be the first of anything. She was the one who suggested using a real hurricane as backdrop. A modern-day Oya, violet robes swirling around her, her machete raised to cut the storm in pieces. No CGI. No retouching. No one else would dare. *It was a mistake*, Maite pleaded to the pantheon of goddesses painted on her mother's ceiling. *My mom didn't really want to be there. It was her reflection that caused her to go. That other LaZuli.* The LaZuli in the scrying mirror who lived on the other side. The LaZuli who demanded adoration, the LaZuli who walked with the dead. *She* was the reason her mother now walked among them. Without that other LaZuli, Maite believed, her mother would still be alive.

How to grieve someone who pierced the veil of death and always came back? Did it work the other way, could LaZuli scratch the scrim of reality from the other side and appear in a bird or a teacup? Maite believed yes. She wore her mother's velvet shawls like a skin and slept with her tarot underneath her pillow, positioning the cards like words to a spell that might conjure her mother's ghost in her dreams. The pantry and fridge held enough ingredients for Maite to make her mother's favorite meals, which she cooked once each a day, hoping the scent of coconut rice and frozen orange chicken would coax her mother's spirit to join her at the table. Alone in the house they had shared, Maite entombed herself in her mother's bedroom and waited for inanimate objects to reveal a message, to reassure her that she was not alone. She couldn't even bury Maria Lucia's remains; the toxic waters and aggressive alligators made it impossible to retrieve the bodies. To be closer to her, Maite collected nail clippings from the floor of her bathroom and pulled clumps of hair from her bristle brush. Using shredded strips of her mother's pillowcase, Maite stitched a mushroom-sized pouch for her mother's keratin remains and tied off the gris-gris bag with a gold chain. She wore it around her neck and stacked her mother's onyx and amber rings on her own thick fingers. She'd stare outside the window, drumming her fingers against the back of the burgundy velvet couch, the soft thuds a metronome for her looping thoughts. This wasn't the way it was supposed to go, there must have been some mistake. Maria Lucia would've known, must've known, that she was in danger. Especially if she knew the hurricane would claim her, why didn't she say goodbye? Maite knew there were answers, but with her mother gone, there was no one to guide her to the underworld. Until she met me.

My name is Maria Caracol. I live in Aguamictlan with a fat black cat who hunts beetles off the maracuya vines unfurling from my husband's grave. Our palette is overwhelmingly—frighteningly—green. Moss and tendrils, vines and fronds. The resilient ashy pigeons and emerald parrots bathe themselves in stormwater trapped in the fake Olmec head fountain down the street. Remnants of steel train tracks peek through the earthquake-shattered cement like embedded fossils. Aguamictlan was once home to the big cats of Balam and is the only place you can still find the hallucinogenic Golden Chalice; the rare yellow flowers sprout from the cracks in the sidewalk and creep up our useless street signs. For most people, eating the flowers straight from the vine can be lethal. Like Lafcadio with venomous snakes, I am immune to the toxicity of the Golden Chalice. One of the books I saved from the library summed up resentment like this: *It's like drinking poison and waiting for someone else to die.* When I take the poison, someone else dies.

There used to be a book in the Aguamictlan Public Library, sandwiched between the *Popol Vuh* and the *Twilight* series, that could explain who I am. Its pages are now either burned or covered in capybara pee, one of the thousands of books we couldn't save. The day before the Orion Earthquake, the city leaders announced the closing of our town's only library. *For our protection,* the mayor had said, subconsciously motioning to the city officials standing behind him. But chaos doesn't recognize a difference between *us* and *them*. More of *us* than *them* survived, and all of *them* fled Aguamictlan to the calm coast of the north or the deserted mountains in the east. *We* couldn't leave.

During the days of the earth resettling, Set and I survived off our emergency kits and, after their burial rites, the kits of our neighbors. We witnessed the lingering pyrocumulus clouds and swirling wet winds from the restless Pacific creating monsoons that swept away our crumbled streets. Abrupt aftershocks triggered fires in North Aguamictlan, and the riots created a tear gas over Rio de los Santos. Even if we had wanted to leave, we couldn't. Fires to the north, the wild river and riots to the west, military to the south, and the hungry panthers of Balam roaming our streets. Set and I spent the year of transition crouched against the window that faced the lawn, wrapped in our bedsheets and blankets. As long as the two of us agreed on our reality, we could survive the terrors we did not understand and could not predict. We told each other small fictions to keep our minds from breaking: The house across the street had not been burned out, it was covered with an insulating black cocoon and would soon regenerate wood and cement. The viejita who sold flowers on the corner had not picked up a live wire with her hand, she had moved to Osaka on an Ikebana fellowship. That is not a mountain lion with a tattooed arm in her jaws. It is a mountain lion desperate to feed her cubs.

Before they executed him, Set was an engineer for the Balam Wildlife Refuge & Botanical Gardens. Founded by a misanthropic cat lady who resisted both the pleas of luxury developers and community protests to convert the land to housing, the Aguamictlan sanctuary housed over a hundred big cats rescued from exotic pet dealers and downsized millionaires. Balam was once considered *the* tourist destination for Southern California nature lovers, and Set designed and built animatronic butterflies as part of the park's environmental activations. They ranged from the size of a rose petal to the size of a school bus. During the day, the solar-powered wings opened and closed to simulate a butterfly flitting around a flower. Twilight and particularly cloudy days paralyzed the butterflies, yet they were just as marvelous to observe. I believe if ever the sun breaks through that canopy of untended trees, the creatures made by my husband's hands will revive. Over twenty-five hundred species of flora and fauna native to different areas of Central and South America had thrived in that contained jungle. Now the creatures and rabid plants rule over our entire town.

Years before Orion turned everything to rubble and rot, Set and I visited Chile to attend the Duendes y Hadas Literary Festival, where I attended a panel discussion on the Tuatha dé Danann and took a workshop on arctic poetry. On our way back to the hotel after attending a keynote on flexible narration, Set and I walked through a Santiago park crowded with couples lounging on the grass. We held hands and dreamily, naïvely, asked, *Could we live here? They have a farmers' market. There wouldn't be another military dictatorship, right? At least not so soon. Right? We could live here. Uruguay seems chill, too.*

We joined a growing group of people watching an open-air play. Actors in striking black-and-white-and-red-patterned costumes stood holding hands in a circle around a towering hut. It was a performance about the Selk'nam, an indigenous tribe who once lived on the southernmost tip of Chile. The last butterfly Set made was modeled after the Selk'nam spirits cloaked in a pattern of black-and-white stripes and red dots. It is at the front entrance of Balam, right next to the ticket booth, fully intact.

The Portuguese word for butterfly is borboleta. Like tecolote, ñandutí, and kitsune, it is one of my favorite words to say aloud. Borboleta. Borbo-leta. Bor-bo-le-ta. I learned it from Natalia. When she found me on the night of the caimans, we first spoke to each other in fractured English and Portuñol. She eventually took over the house next door to mine, which is to say she is my only neighbor. We are the only two humans in this part of Aguamictlan, which is to say we are safe. We survive on the fresh eggs from her chickens and the abundant fruit trees I tend. We take any excess to the other side of the town for the viejitos, sometimes they will give us capybara meat or patched-together blankets for trade. I taught Natalia how to fold paper into shapes and how to bind a book using cardboard box scraps and shredded plastic bags as thread. She helped bring me back to life, but is not responsible for anything I've done since. Like Natalia, I once had a sister.

If you tarot: My sister embodied a twisted Empress and the most callous aspects of the Magician. If you don't tarot: My sister believed her psychic gifts entitled her to adoration, fame, and riches. I believe that actively pursuing fame is like inviting a destructive enemy to inhabit your body. Unlike the Tower card's cleansing fire and necessary ruin, egomania is a rot.

Maria Lucia and I were born twins but only shared the moment of birth. Her face is a heart and mine is an egg. My hair is straight and so black that it shines blue, and her curly crown had a golden sheen like our mother's. She saw futures that were limitless in potential outcomes. I could only see the past and deep interiors. The ghosts wanted to talk to me, the time travelers preferred her. When we were thirteen years old, my sister adopted a stage name and began to cultivate her otherworldly identity. She bought an earlobe-stretching kit and reshaped her skin to make room for our grandfather's lapis lazuli cuff links. The deep blue square stones against her copper skin made her face look like an unearthed burial mask. She renamed herself LaZuli and read tarot for our classmates. I made the mistake of still referring to her by her family name, MariLuz, and the even graver mistake of sitting next to her and reading the palms of our friends who trusted their own skin over a deck of cards. What I considered a sister side business quickly became a competition in MariLuz's eyes. Who could do more readings in a forty-five-minute lunch break? Who would get the rockeros and who would get the cheerleaders? Who would pretend to be friends with us and tell us all their secrets, then never look us in the eye again because we knew too much? I had stepped on her territory, but I didn't think it was that important. Reading fortunes was just an easy way to make snack money and get good chisme. But MariLuz soon broke off from our tag-team divination and sat at a lunch table on the opposite side of the outdoor quad. Without my sister next to me, I got dizzy spells and headaches after each reading. I complained to her about it. *Palm reading is too much touching*, she said. *Who knows what you are picking up?*

One day the pain was so bad I fainted while sharpening my pencil. I hit my head on the edge of the teacher's metal desk and the ambulance came for me. Eleven stitches, right across the middle of my forehead. MariLuz knelt next to my bed and her hands cast a shadow over my bandaged forehead.

You shouldn't do this anymore, Mari, she said in that raspy whisper her future clients would call ethereal. *There is another path for you. I'll take care of your clients while you recover.*

I agreed, relieved that my injury would give me a few days to rest. She tugged on her lapis lazuli earrings and slightly turned her head, just enough so I could see her smile. She always had to be the only one. It was after my recovery that I'd noticed she'd started clipping me out of family photos. Then began the interruptions, talking over me at dinner and ignoring my questions as if I weren't there. I became invisible to her, or, as my grandfather said, she killed me off without the mess. I retreated into my mushroom teas and ghosts and watched LaZuli rise.

If I don't count the commercials or the few times I clicked over to watch snippets of her morning show, I saw my sister only twice after she left the house when we turned sixteen. The first time was when she came back to Aguamictlan for our grandfather's entierro. We were twenty-five years old. I had just started working on my *Book of Marias* and MariLuz had recently appeared as a card reader in the remake of *Live and Let Die*. She showed up to the secluded hill where my grandfather wanted to be buried wearing a lime-green caped dress and oversized sunglasses that made her look like a praying mantis. She left a monstrous bouquet at the head of his freshly dug grave, the thick burgundy ribbon tied around the stems dangling into the pit. We said nothing to each other as we lowered his silk-wrapped body into the earth. I pulled the petals off the red roses and stacked them on top of each other, one petal for each year of his life, and bound them with the delicate gold chain he always wore around his neck. MariLuz tossed in heaps of peat moss and scattered quetzal feathers over the spongy sphagnum. She said nothing as we arranged the remaining flowers and feathers, the gold-wrapped petals and obsidian sphere, a miniature bottle of his favorite mezcal. We lit the votive candles and burned his prayers as instructed, then tossed the flaming papelitos into the pit. MariLuz and I stepped back. A small explosion, a fragrant crackling. I quieted the fire with moist dirt from Balam that Set had scooped up for me, full of bugs and spores. MariLuz poured in a bucket of ocean water. We repeated this, layering the dirt and water until the hole disappeared.

When we finished the entierro, we faced each other. I wasn't sure if she was even looking at me because of those ridiculous sunglasses and I readied myself for an attack that never came—MariLuz didn't want the house, his chucherías, his furniture. Nothing. She didn't want anything I had. Her idea of worth was on a light spectrum I couldn't see. Still, I opened my mouth and screamed. A long and sharp wail to empty the sadness from my body. When I opened my eyes, she had simply placed her hand on her hip. The bitch wouldn't even grant me a smirk. I turned and walked away.

The last time I saw my sister was right after Set died. She showed up to the house we grew up in, the house our grandfather left me, the home I shared with Set. From my bedroom, I heard rustling in the kitchen and furniture scraping the floors. I didn't bother investigating, unconcerned about capybaras searching for food or survivors seeking supplies. As long as they left me alone, I didn't care who came in and what they took. MariLuz revealed herself when she sent her five-year-old daughter into my dark room with a cup of ginger tea and dry toast. The little girl looked like us. Draw the Mayan glyph for zero and those are our eyes, the eyes inherited from our grandfather that let us see into other worlds. As dark as cacao seeds, and as infinite as 0. Keeping with our maternal tradition, my sister named her daughter Maria. Maria Teresa Milfuegos. I could see the girl's unnamed father in her chiseled cheeks and freckles. *I didn't love him*, my sister said. *Not the way you loved Set.* That was the closest my sister came to expressing sympathy. She switched out my pillow for one that was dry and clean, and then sat at the edge of my bed. Every time I opened my eyes, she was there. She looked like herself, less like LaZuli with that stupid Cleopatra wig and caked-on glitter. My mind and body had split from each other and from the world, but I do remember hearing MariLuz encourage her daughter to draw the wild animals of Aguamictlan to pass the time. Of course, MariLuz wasn't there for me or her daughter. When my body and mind finally reconnected, I discovered MariLuz had stolen my unfinished *Book of Marias* and our grandfather's obsidian rings. The last words she ever said to me were, *Stay in the shadows.* I dove into their beckoning black.

A week after LaZuli's death, on the eve of her thirteenth birthday, Maite was forced to remember me. Wrapped in her mother's shawls, she pressed her face against the frosted glass of the front window and watched a pair of pastel power suits walk the snaking path through the massive magueys and prickly pear cacti to her front door. Ciro Acosta and his wife, Clara, had arrived to finalize her mother's death.

Ciro arranged his slender silver computer and briefcase on the glass kitchen table while Clara walked around the house with her tablet, photographing and cataloging the contents of Maria Lucia's life. Maite didn't care about what happened to all those things; she had already taken the rings and hairbrushes, the shawls and silk scarves that had belonged to her mom. They were safe, stuffed inside a pillowcase on her own bed. Everything else belonged to LaZuli.

Ciro opened his silver briefcase and slid a thick black envelope across the table. Maite's full name was written across the top of the security seal.

"What is this for?"

"Your mother instructed us to share this with you in the event of her death."

Maite shifted under Ciro's stare. His gray eyes and too-small pupils had always made her uneasy. *Click, click* went the digital shutter of Clara's tablet. Maite had once seen LaZuli practice emotions in the mirror before a meeting with the Acostas. Watching the seamless shift from joy to sorrow to rage to fright had made Maite wary of her own mother's face. Anytime her mom laughed with her or punctuated her apologies with tears, Maite considered it might've just been a dress rehearsal for a negotiation or a prophetic performance. Although she couldn't see the future or visit the past the way we could, Maite did inherit a portion of our family's animal instinct and watery intuition. As she watched the baby-blue and pink lawyers run their eyes and hands over all the surfaces of her home, Maite sensed that she was again in the presence of people who knew how to make their faces and bodies tell lies.

Maite pressed her thumb against the seal and opened the package. Inside, my leather-bound *Book of Marias* and a faded picture of me and MariLuz as kids getting ready to trick-or-treat. We each held up plastic jack-o'-lantern heads with lopsided smiles. MariLuz wore a burgundy leotard and a skirt made of fabric remnants and mismatched scarves; she had safety-pinned little bells and beads to the edges, so when she walked it sounded like she was shimmering. In her hand, she held a grapefruit wrapped in aluminum foil—her crystal ball. I dressed up as a black cat and drew whiskers on my face with a marker that smelled like black licorice. I taped paper clips to my fingers and called them claws, swiping anyone who I considered a threat. What Maite couldn't see in that Halloween picture was our grandfather and his gap-toothed smile behind the camera.

"Is this my mom's sister?"

"Twin sister," said Clara.

"Your mother named you as the main beneficiary of her assets. But since you are only twelve—"

"I'm thirteen tomorrow."

"Happy birthday," Ciro and Clara said. Ciro continued, "Your mother's profession opens up a series of complications surrounding her death. It is in your best interest if you trust us, just like your mother trusted us, to figure all this out."

"What complications? She died in Hurricane Julia, along with all those other people who couldn't get out of the storm in time."

"*Couldn't* or wouldn't? See, that is what we have no way of knowing for certain and are working on clarifying in the courts."

Clara cleared her throat and glared at Ciro before softening her gaze to address Maite. "Don't worry about the details, Maite. It's grown-up stuff."

"She's my mother. I have a right to know."

Clara took a seat next to Ciro. "The question is, do we protect her psychic legacy or her celebrity assets?"

"Meaning, if your mom knew she was going to die, and didn't warn the people who followed her to New Orleans, knowing the hurricane would ultimately kill her, she is responsible for their deaths as well."

"That's stupid. It was an accident."

"Your mother predicted the discovery of a pyramid in Oklahoma and the independence of Tibet. Down to the date. Public opinion is that she had real psychic power."

"She did," Maite muttered. The lawyers were in the same position as she was. Bewildered that LaZuli, an otherwise fastidious psychic, wouldn't even hint at her impending death. Or at the very least provide postmortem guidance to navigate the ensuing administrative and emotional inconveniences. "What happens to me now?"

"Typically care is provided by the last living relative."

"I don't know my dad." Maite looked down at the book. "My aunt barely exists to me."

"Your mother was estranged from her sister. We will do all we can to find her. In the meantime, we can't leave you alone here. Many of LaZuli's followers are not rational."

Clara snorted. "That's a dangerous understatement."

Maite had already seen rumors circulating about her mom's face appearing in the colorful suds of LaZuli's Reflective Bath Orbs, and just that morning she had read a chilling online discussion on how LaZuli could be resurrected. If only they had access to her DNA.

"So where do I go now?"

Ciro and Clara glanced at each other. "With us."

Maite watched her mother's house shrink and disappear from the rear window of Ciro and Clara's self-driving SUV. She sprawled out on the wide backseat and rested her head against the silver duffel bag that contained the remnants of her life. As the car descended the winding roads leading out of Crescent Moon Bay, her ears popped with the change in elevation. Ciro and Clara continued working, sitting across from each other on plush gray seats with a small oval table in between them. Cataloged images of her mother's house flashed on and off Clara's tablet screen. In the SUV's front window, Maite saw armed guards wearing mirrored sunglasses wave the car through, and they exited the final tunnel out of her hometown. On the opposing side of traffic, guards blocked a car that was covered in sigils and holographic eyes and triangles, symbols of her mother's most devoted fanatics.

"It's about five hours until we reach Rio," said Ciro. "I'm turning on the comfortable transport." The air conditioner hummed on and the windows darkened. A spritz of oxytocin-infused air freshener filled the backseat. Maite dozed off wondering where she would be at that moment if LaZuli's fans had reached her before the Acostas had.

Neon lights strobed in her dreams. Maite opened her eyes to flashing billboards promising new buildings, and the skeletons of half-built skyscrapers. A trio of pigeons nested in the rubble. Like Aguamictlan, Rio was deemed uninhabitable after Orion. The earthquake had transformed the once-inland city to a ruined coastal land, or "lucrative opportunity," if you suffered from wealth and its opportunistic visions. The waves of the Pacific Ocean lapped at the edges of what used to be Rio de los Santos, or as it was once referred to by the locals: D. Los or SanTown. It would soon be renamed Perla del Mar to bury its urban past and highlight its new seaside future.

Clara had taken off her heels and sat next to Ciro, both of them facing the side windows.

"It's a miracle what a little investment can do," said Ciro, rubbing Clara's ankles. "Well, not exactly *little*." He laughed and Clara laughed and Maite wondered how much of their smugness could be credited to LaZuli's fortune. The SUV continued past a block of glass and steel buildings, past the fluorescent green cafés and murals depicting lush trees and bright flowers, seemingly the only greenery in the city. Torn white posters with names and faces stuck to the side of a wall. Maite squinted, *MISSING* was the only word she could make out. The vehicle slowed to a stop in front of what looked like a perforated giant aluminum soup can, a cylindrical silver building with rectangle and square windows dotting its surface. Clara smiled wide, the flashing blue and red neon lights of the overhead billboard reflecting on her white teeth. "Welcome home."

Maite's new bare white room was nothing like the bedroom she'd painted and decorated herself. The only color came from the neon streetlights flooding through the rectangular floor-to-ceiling window overlooking the empty street. Next to the window, a wide and clean square bed with one single pillow. A black eye mask and bottle of water rested on the aluminum nightstand. Ciro and Clara's window faced the ocean, which they could still see clearly beyond a mile of vacant lots. Clara showed Maite the white wardrobe and matching drawers where Maite could store the few leggings and sweaters she brought along with her. Maite nodded and held on to her silver bag, unable to ignore the twinge of her intuition telling her that she wouldn't be there for too long. The attached bathroom contained a waterless toilet and a glass-bowl sink balanced atop a wide metal cabinet. Clara showed her how to work the hand pump to draw the water down from the massive tank above the building. Until the desalination plant was completed, Clara explained, the new residents of Rio took part in the state's monthly water auctions and they were *always* among the top bidders. They had more clean water than they even needed! So they kept it in tanks scattered around the developing city. Stark room and spare furnishings aside, Maite didn't miss the Bay. Anyplace she inhabited would only be a shell.

Maite figured out how to operate the levers on the shower and stepped into the granite-and-glass cube. *Grateful*, she thought as the hot water rained on her head. She was grateful for Ciro and Clara. The cloudiness of the past week started to fade and dissolve in the steam. She inhaled deep, the scent of the eucalyptus and peppermint soap felt like a cool waterfall in her lungs. Clean and refreshed, Maite dried off and wrapped her long brown hair into two cone-shaped buns on each side of her head. She would thank Ciro and Clara as soon as they returned from their rooftop dinner party. They had made the plans months ago with their neighbors. *Very exclusive, adults only*. But, they said as they walked out the door, they would bring back a dessert for her birthday. An *exquisite* crème brûlée made with real emu eggs. The electronic door lock whirred behind them

Maite wrapped herself in her mother's violet shawl and stretched out on the aqua leather couch in the pink and palm-treed living room. She watched the shifting colors of the neon lights until she couldn't keep her eyes open anymore. The hum of the generator lulled her into a deep sleep.

If there were any survivors, they'd say the dinner party was *memorable*. They'd only remember the sound because they would still be in denial about what they saw. Clinking wine-glasses, then plates crashing. Wooden chairs falling over, bodies landing on top of each other. Shouts and screams. Dark teal emu eggs rolling on the floor—their thick yolks a cream down my throat.

The sound of rolling wheels and a rhythmic clanging somewhere in the building jolted Maite awake. Startled by her bright surroundings, she held her breath until she remembered where she was. She lifted her head and wiped the drool from the corner of her mouth. "Ciro?" Silence. Maite washed her face in her bathroom. Two new pimples had been born overnight, one in the middle of her chin and the other hugging her left nostril. For an instant Maite regretted not packing any of LaZuli's White Clay Milagros Masque. She dried her face and wondered if her hosts had a stockpile of LaZuli's products. "Clara?"

Maite knocked on Ciro and Clara's bedroom door. It swayed open under her touch. The bed was made and empty. The thick blue line of the ocean was visible from their large rectangular window and Maite walked in for a better look. That's when she saw, three stories below, a cluster of white vans and silver motorcycles from the interstate law enforcement. Maite jumped back away from the window. She peeked over again, careful. The uniformed officers pointed at the rows of gurneys draped in white sheets—underneath, the topography of human bodies. Thin red slashes seeped up through the sheets. She counted twelve gurneys. Maite couldn't hear what they were saying but she did hear the faint sound of footsteps approaching. On her tiptoes, Maite raced back to the living room and grabbed her duffel bag, then ran back to her bedroom to pick up her sneakers and dirty clothes she'd tossed on the floor. One loud bang against the apartment's metal door, and then the whir of an electronic lock. Maite bolted to the only place she knew she could hide. She folded herself into the cabinet underneath the bathroom sink, holding tight to her things, trying to quiet her thrashing heartbeat to keep it from giving her away.

The officers entered her room. She heard the click of a lighter and the smell of cigarette smoke. "That's everyone. Took out the whole building."

"It won't be empty long."

Their husky laughter trailed off as they exited the room. Maite breathed slowly through her nose, waiting for their voices and the smell of smoke to dissipate. When the door finally clanged shut, she unfolded herself and pushed out of the cramped cabinet. Her back ached and her sweat-damp clothes clung to her body. She peeked out from her room's rect-angular window to watch the last of the motorcycles pull away, the bright morning sun glinting off their chrome helmets.

Once again, Maite was alone. The murder (massacre?) of the Acostas wasn't something she could even consider with-out dissolving into a panic, so she switched on the survival mode she'd developed growing up under LaZuli. Her mother had a tendency to shut out her hired staff—she never trusted anyone after a personal chef leaked images of toddler Maite to the tabloids—and she would leave her daughter alone for days at a time, convincing Maite that she was a *big girl!* who could *handle anything!* While LaZuli performed for packed stadi-ums across the country or read fortunes on a yacht for a bach-elorette party en route to Rosarito, Maite learned to operate as a girl without past or future, to suppress all fear and hope and become a strictly biological being who only needed water, sleep, and the occasional protein.

The building's air conditioner powered down with a loud whir. Maite fanned herself, cracking open a window in the living room to let in a ribbon of breeze. The officers had not only shut down the generator, they had taken all the fresh food and nearly cleared out the dry goods, leaving only the peanut butter, a can of tomato paste, and a package of spotted beans which Maite set aside. She took out the trays of ice from the freezer and poured the cubes into a glass pitcher, then refilled the trays from the kitchen faucet. Sipping on the cold water, she found stale bread wrapped in foil and made a couple of peanut butter sandwiches for her trek. She pulled a buttoned shirt off the hangers from Ciro's side of the closet and a lavender velvet blazer from Clara's side because it felt good to take something of theirs. Maite used one of Ciro's socks to wipe down everything she thought she had touched, and rearranged the clothes and food in her duffel bag so it would all fit. She sat still on the Acostas' aqua leather couch, and, not wanting to further contaminate the place with her fingerprints and sweat, she waited for the sun to go down. *Grateful*, she repeated to herself. Grateful to Ciro for leaving his car keys in his baby-blue suit pocket, hanging neatly on the back of an armchair. Grateful that she had a way out. Needing a distraction from her racing mind, Maite flipped open my book of Marias. An origami crane fell out of the pages and onto the floor. She picked it up and tucked it back into my stories.

SEA OF SORROW:
QUEENS, MYSTICS, & ANTAGONISTS

by Maria Caracol

THE FIRST MARIA

MARY MAGDALENE

THE VIRGIN MARY

LA MALINCHE

BLOODY MARY

~~MARÍA DE LOS SANTOS~~   *Machete Maria!*

MARY SHELLEY

MARIE LAVEAU I AND II

MARIE CURIE

MARÍA SABINA

LA INDIA MARÍA

MARIA DEL MAR

*I don't like the title, Mari.
You also need an introduction. Explain how you get high
and talk to all these dead bitches. Don't leave yourself
out of the story.*

MARÍA DE LOS SANTOS

INSIDE A GIANT OPAL EGG on the edge of a swamp lived María de los Santos. A silver and black iron staircase coiled around its smooth exterior like a python. The sludgy waters filled with reptiles and relentless rains kept María confined to what her husband called a palace, what María called a prison, what remains a grave.

We won't always be alone here, Francisco promised his young wife. *Just as soon as my workers finish building the city on the other side of the river, we will have the family you've always wanted. Soon, María. Soon.* María pressed the jagged ruby on her ring with her thumb to keep from asking what soon meant. Francisco meticulously parted his hair above the sharp arch of his right eyebrow. The part was so severe and clean that María could see his scalp turn blood-red whenever she, or anyone, dared question him. He prepared his stiff leather satchel for another trip west toward the coast she longed to see, his glass of wine untouched and the velvet ribbons of her corset fastened tight.

María daydreamed of having a life like her sisters, happy and buoyant with their hunter husbands, surrounded by their laughing children. But María was the adventurous one, the one who fell in love with Francisco de los Santos, captain of a ship sailing to the Americas from Spain. She had heard stories of how he had traveled up the great snake of the Amazon and picked up servants like souvenirs. When he returned to Spain to pick up more men for his latest conquest in the New World, he saw María and decided he needed her. María, barely sixteen and wanting nothing more in her young life than to be needed. She didn't listen to her mother's warnings that she would never see them again, that Fernando wasn't the type for sentimental trips across the ocean. And now her mother's warnings taunted her. Fernando's ambition to build a city kept him miles away on most days, leaving María in the sole company of Iara, Fernando's longtime servant. Iara lived in a box-shaped stone house between the Egg and the low stone wall encircling the de los Santos property. Desperate for companionship, María spent the daylight hours outdoors alongside Iara, inviting the insects to crawl over her chunky citrine rings and amber necklaces while she watched Iara chase away the snakes and small lizards with her gleaming silver machete. María followed Iara around the Egg as she worked, comforted by the sound of the beaded bracelets adorning Iara's ankles and wrists. Through pantomime and words María had never heard before but quickly learned, Iara shared stories she had collected in her forced journey through the Americas. María learned about man-eating fish and desert devils with giant horns between their legs. Of flayed gods and celestial-bodied women. At first María, full of wonder, vowed to pass on Iara's stories of enchanted snakes and rivers to her own children. But as time passed and Fernando's visits became so spare and touchless that he seemed an apparition floating through the Egg and back out the door, the imprint of horseshoes the only evidence he'd been there, María grew resentful hearing about children who were born of mud or sprang forth fully formed to battle for their mothers' honor. In Fernando's extended absence, María's desire to be a mother festered inside of her, growing into something dark and heavy. She withdrew from Iara, and grew jealous of the bugs crawling all over each other in the garden, torn between cradling and destroying the beetle eggs she found buried in the wet dirt.

Then the rains came, further driving María into the shadows of the Egg. The swamp spilled over the low stone wall and saturated the garden. Bats and finicky yellow birds pecked at the swelling fruit trees. Crocodiles climbed out of their swamp over the low stone wall to gather plant matter and mud to build nests for their smooth eggs. Iara kept the animals and insects from entering the de los Santos house, but she could not stop the invasive tendrils and flowers of the Golden Chalice vine from curling up the stairs and pressing up against María's bedroom window, tempting her. The repressed hatred she carried for Francisco circulated in her body, causing the festering sludge within María to harden in her veins. Her darkness had a voice, and it sounded like her mother saying, *Niña abandonada,* it sounded like murmured melodic reassurances that her fate was to eat handfuls of the Golden Chalice flower until she felt weak and dreamy. Her breath would slow and her eyelids would grow heavy. Then, the dark voice said, she must feed her useless body to the crocodile and her hatchlings. Then and only then would her body give life.

María sat in her claw-footed tub and poured water over her head with a giant conch shell given to her by Iara. *Dime cocodrilo, que dices cocodrilo,* she sang, asking the crocodiles to speak. She rose from the water and stepped out into her room, dripping on the stone floor as she walked around her bedroom, collecting her jewels and heirlooms. Barefoot, she walked outside and descended the coiled iron stairs wearing every emerald, garnet, sapphire, and precious stone she owned around her fingers and neck. A magnificent rainbow of gems reflected against María's bare skin as she severed the lethal Golden Chalice from their vines with the jagged edges of her ruby ring. She collected the delicate petals in her cupped palm.

On her way to the crocodile's grotto, she noticed flickering candlelight and restless shadows dancing against the walls of Iara's room. Curious, María approached the open window and peered inside, careful to avoid tipping the lit candle. The strange man's suntanned skin carried the smell of the sea. Black bands and indecipherable letters covered the mountains of muscles on his back. Iara's hands gripped his arms and the dark voice in María's head quieted. María now heard Iara's languid moans and the rumbling breaths of her lover. María wanted to have that heat for herself. She clenched the yellow flowers in one hand, and with the other dipped her fingers in the pooled candle. The wax burned her flesh, bringing all her senses back to life and dissolving the heavy darkness in her veins. The wet dirt between her toes, the incessant chirping of the crickets, the trickle of evening mist seeping into her hair. María felt it all. Iara looked into María's eyes and parted her mouth. An invitation to join them. María entered the room. The deadly yellow flowers sank into the dirt.

The story of that night sailed back and forth across the Pacific Ocean and shape-shifted with every retelling. By the time Iara taught María how to wield the machete and understand the uses of all her plants, the tattooed sailor's story traveled to the edges of the river and rubbed against the tongues of Francisco's workers. In one version, the bold sailor triumphantly wrestled a pair of wild crocodiles to death with his bare hands, breaking an old witch's curse and revealing two eager beauties, hungry to please their savior in their egg-shaped palace. This was the story Francisco de los Santos overheard. Egg-shaped palace. His skin turned red and his eyes widened to empty black pools. After years of neglect, Francisco finally returned to his wife.

Iara was ready for her body to die. The body she lived in had been captured and passed from the Amazon through the Chaco, up and down the Andes, sailed across the ocean to the pyramids, through forests and deserts, until it ended up in the hands of Francisco. And now she stood in front of the wooden door of the Egg, watching Francisco descend from his horse, his eyes fixed on the house and a faint red glow radiating from his hands. Iara had found an unlikely apprentice in María de los Santos. She hadn't taught her everything, just enough to give her a fighting chance.

Iara stepped toward Francisco to meet him face-to-face. Even in the moonlight, she could see the veiny ribbons protruding from his neck. She looked him in the eyes and insulted him in a language she knew he understood. Francisco wrapped his hands around Iara's throat, tightening his grip until her body went limp. He heaved her over his shoulder and threw her body over the low stone wall, where the crocodiles and snakes pulled her into the water in a flurry of thrashes and waves.

María opened her eyes. Iara was gone.

She heard the thrashing in the water, she smelled Fernando's tobacco. María de los Santos rose from her bed and walked to the top of the winding stairs, observing the frothing water and the sounds of cracking bone. She dug her nails into the handle of the machete. A deep croak escaped from her throat. Francisco turned away from his kill and looked up at his wife. Maria tightened her grip on the blade. "*María*," he said. He raised one of his hands and beckoned her down. María did not move. He made his way through the mud and climbed the stairs, one step at a time, hands behind his back, never breaking his stare. He reached the top, his grip on the smooth rock tightening. In one swift strike, María raised the machete and severed Francisco's head from his body.

Francisco's head watched María as she poured cold water over her shoulders with Iara's conch shell. She sang as the blood washed away: *Ay, cocodrilo, mi querido cocodrilo.* When she rose from the tub, the water had turned a bright rose-red. María hummed as she slipped all her rings over her bruised fingers once again. *Ay cocodrilo, mi querido cocodrilo.* Gold chains wrapped around her neck and waist. *¿Quién soy yo, cocodrilo?* Abalone combs and clips embedded in her wet hair. *Dime cocodrilo.* A rose-shaped garnet hat pin, pierced through her ear. *Mi querido cocodrilo.* María descended the stairs holding Francisco by his sleek black hair. She walked through Iara's garden and past the low stone wall, where Francisco's horse reared on its hind legs and galloped away. María followed in the horse's wake through the path that led out of the swampy forest. The slimy sharp stones cut her feet. When she was tired of walking, María set Francisco's head on the ground. She stepped back and watched the night creatures devour her husband's remains.

Just before sunrise, María returned to the Egg. She sat on the low stone wall wearing all her jewelry like a second skin and gazed at the still, dark water below her feet. There was no sign of Iara or her remains. María pulled the garnet hat pin from her ear and tossed it down. The water rippled and its deadly creatures rose to the surface. The caimans gathered, looking up at the creamy flesh of the woman above, waiting. A groan filled the swamp as a near-translucent crocodile rose and opened its massive jaws. María asked, *Tell me crocodile. Who am I, crocodile?*

Sepaktli, the chorus of caimans answered. *Keeper of this water's secret.*

Sepaktli, María repeated her new name. *Sepaktli.* She stepped into the open jaws of the crocodile, and descended into the swamp.

Mari, why isn't this the first story in your book?

Aguamictlan should be first. It's our home.

The Mimilocas hunted under the new moon. The trio crawled and contorted their bodies across the sharp concrete and stalactite steel remains of the Rio Mictlan bridge to scour the streets of Rio de los Santos for discarded treasures. Like Maite, the Mimilocas were born in the destruction of Orion and its aftermath. Children of a flailing earth! From nothing, they made all. Sleeping bags from rain tarps, water filters from screen doors. Bombs from car parts.

Maite, after performing her own midnight acrobatics to escape the third floor of a sealed crime scene, hadn't expected to confront a trio of strangers sitting inside Ciro's SUV. Through the front window, Maite saw their distorted faces, covered in glossy red and black paint and coin-sized white sequins. She heard muffled laughter, young and crackling. Curiosity took the place of shock and Maite stepped closer for a better look. The laughter stopped, and their eyes locked on to her. Immediately the group filed out of the car. They were dressed in solid black, but the heavy silver chains and blades in their hands glinted in the neon light.

Maite gripped the straps of her bag and stepped back as the trio stepped forward. She could see them sneering, smelled the smokiness on their clothes.

"Where the fuck'd you come from?"

"Crescent Moon Bay."

"Explains the moon shoes." Maite looked down at her iridescent high-tops. *Moon shoes?*

They circled in closer, pressing Maite against the aluminum wall. The Mimilocas pinched the sleeve of her silver windbreaker. "You lose your jet pack on the way down here?"

"*I* believe you're from the moon. Just look at those craters on your face."

They jabbed their elbows at each other and laughed.

Maite flinched. "I'm trying . . . I was trying to get back home." She touched her face, then pointed up at the empty building. "Everyone's gone."

"You shouldn't be here."

"I know."

"What's in the space bag?"

They snatched the silver duffel bag out of Maite's hands and opened the zipper. They sniffed the contents and looked at Maite, their eyes wide and expectant. "Is this peanut butter?"

The approaching rumble of a passing cement truck sent the Mimilocas scrambling to a nearby construction site, taking Maite's bag with them. Maite chased after them and hid from the truck's beaming headlights behind a hulking excavator, a hill of crumbled brick under its static claw. From this angle, Maite could see what remained of Ciro's SUV. No tires, no passenger-side door. And if Maite's quick scan of what the Mimilocas had in their frayed denim bag was correct, no navigational interface.

"The car was already jacked when we got here," they said. They fished out the foil-wrapped packet and handed the duffel bag back to Maite. "Mostly." The Mimilocas leaned against the giant wheels of the construction vehicle and devoured the sandwiches. Maite watched them eat, feeling calm despite the crude weapons at their sides. She'd felt more uneasy with the Acostas. When they finished eating, the Mimilocas wiped the smears of peanut butter from their mouths, unintentionally removing a bit of makeup from their faces. "If you're trying to leave Rio, you can probably catch a ride," they said. "You're dressed rich enough. One of the construction workers around here, the lady ones, might feel sorry for you. You have ID?"

"No," Maite lied. Anyone she asked for help would see her name and address and want to know how she got here, who she was with. They'd ask where she was the night Ciro and Clara and all those people became red-streaked bodies under white sheets. The Mimilocas caught her shiver.

"We don't live here. Rio is adults only," they warned. "Even when it's finished being built, can't see this being a place where things will grow."

A small flood gathered in the corner of Maite's eyes. *What now?*

"My name is Nacho." The Mimiloca with a topknot and soft body placed his hand on Maite's shoulder.

"Nereida," said the tallest Mimiloca with the high ponytail and black triangle painted in the center of her face.

The third Mimiloca, with raised white sequins covering the left side of her face, said nothing. She finished eating her sandwich and neatly folded the foil before sticking it in her back pocket. "You can't stay here," she said. She slung her denim bag over her shoulder and started to walk away. Nacho and Nereida flanked Maite and nudged her forward to join them.

The Mimilocas darted across narrow roads and in between alleys, timing their movements between the flashing of the neon lights. Maite's yellow T-shirt stuck to her skin underneath her navy cardigan with an embroidered orange tabby on the left sleeve. The Mimilocas made Maite take off her space-cadet jacket and throw on something dark over her shirt to help her blend into the night, but there was nothing they could do about her faded baby-blue jeans and holographic sneakers. "I have black paint in the lab," said Nereida. "In case you ever want to come back out for a hunt." Once they were out of range from the glass-and-steel buildings and rumbling trucks, the brightness of Rio dimmed to a pale glow and the Mimilocas moved casually through the blackened and crumbled buildings. Maite's eyes adjusted to the colorless landscape.

"All of this is going to be powder," said Nacho. "I heard they're going to use this machine that will take in all this mess and smash it." He pressed his knuckles together and made a grinding motion. "Pulverized. It's going to be what they use to make sand on their new beach."

Maite stumbled over a raised chunk of asphalt. The third Mimiloca caught her before she fell. "Watch it. The road only gets worse from here."

Nacho helped steady Maite. When Nereida and the third Mimiloca were far enough ahead, Nacho whispered. "That's Burned Betty. She lived through the North Agua-mictlan Fires."

Maite nodded without totally understanding. The fires happened when she was a baby. By the time she was old enough to understand that the world she had inherited was different from the one her mother had grown up in, the North Aguamictlan Fires were something she only heard in casual references to the past, like the extinction of elephants and the Vatican riots.

"The *only* one who survived," Nacho explained.

Burned Betty and Nereida waited for Nacho and Maite to catch up to them at the city's edge, where Rio de los Santos came to an abrupt and jagged end. The remains of the Rio Mictlan bridge stretched before them like a spiky steel caterpillar. Maite teetered to keep her balance. Nacho grabbed Maite's arm. "We've never done this with anyone who isn't us."

"He means you're a risk," said Burned Betty.

"I mean," said Nacho, "we need to know you trust us to get you across. If we say stop, you have to stop moving. One step at the wrong time can send us straight into the hot lava."

"Lava?"

"No," Nerieda said. "It's just mud and shit. Trash from Rio and the rains. But Nacho's right. Don't make it harder for us."

"And don't fall," said Burned Betty. "It'll kill you and we'll have to leave you behind for Machete Maria."

"Who?"

"Machete Maria," said Nacho. "The one who keeps us safe." "Us?"

Nacho pointed to the unseen distance ahead. "Our home."

"We have to trust you, too," said Burned Betty. She tugged at Maite's bag. "That car you wanted to get into definitely wasn't yours, but you had the keys. We haven't asked who brought you here or why you were trying to escape."

Maite didn't offer answers in the long pause that followed.

"We haven't asked you anything," continued Burned Betty, "because your survival here doesn't depend on your past. It's moment-to-moment." She snapped her fingers two, three times. "Do you get it?"

"Yeah," said Maite. She let the silver duffel bag drop from her shoulder, and after making sure the zipper was secure, she looped her arms through each of the hand straps, carrying the bulk of the bag on her back. The *Book of Marias* poked at her spine. Maite rolled her neck and bent her knees, imitating the stance of the Mimilocas. Together, they crossed into Aguamictlan.

The stories that live the longest always involve a quest. The search for gold, for new land, for love, or for the lost. I once went on an underground quest and learned how to resurrect the love of my life. There are worlds of insects and animals underneath the forest floor. Worlds.

Set was murdered holding a hand shovel. The officers said they thought it was a gun—they are trained to say they think everything is a gun—and killed him in front of our home. He should not have died. He should be here with me telling me not to hurt my sister's daughter, which I wouldn't have any need to do if he were not dead.

The viejitos helped me clean and dress my Set in rose oil and wrap him in wide banana leaves. I refused to use the communal burial pit and went against Set's wishes to be laid out in Balam for the jungle and animals to reclaim; I wanted him as close to me as possible. The señoras kept to their old ways and prayed over his body while the rest of us dug a hole in the backyard of the house I shared with Set, right below our bedroom window, for the entierro. We worked together to lower him into the ground. I'm the one who struck the match, but I couldn't throw it in. Señor Ramon's gentle and shaky hand took it from me before it burned my fingertips. A fiery blanket of bright orange and golden red covered Set's body. I wailed and cried until it took on a melody. Eventually, as the sun began to sink, the old men and women who helped me bury my most beloved friend joined my song. Each mourning song was different. Sporadic, staccato, delayed. Someone with a musical mind could notate our grief. On paper, I imagine it would look like scattered ivory teeth and fragments of white bone stuck between layers of black dirt.

When my song quieted to a whisper, La Señora Iris with the blind pit bull handed me a handful of passionfruit seeds wrapped in a swatch of beaded fabric from her old wedding dress. She always wore it on the day we all agreed was Sunday. I covered Set's embers with a thick layer of dirt, then sprinkled in the seeds. The viejitos helped me fill the grave. Despite the elders' warnings, I slept outside.

No wildcats tore me apart, but the next morning, my body was covered in the bites of delicate and deadly spiders. I don't know if it was the reaction to grief or the venom in my veins that caused me to shut down when I returned to our room and rested my head on Set's pillow. I watched the shadows move across the floor and heard the neighbors shuffling outside my door, leaving plates of food and kind notes. My body didn't let me die, we're biologically wired to survive against our will. I sipped from the boxes of water and attended to my basic needs. I saw everything and heard everything. My sister appeared to me in those days, I remember that clearly. She smelled like gardenia and her daughter smelled like crayon. My senses were awake, yet the part of me that generated warmth and life went dormant.

Before Orion: Booming bass of cruising cars; the muted sound of a neighbor practicing drums in their garage; dogs barking at a pair of fat raccoons hiding in a tree; brassy and brazen tamborazos underneath white EZ-Ups; approaching, then fading, sirens; helicopters announcing something no one can hear; cuetes; inappropriate giggling; crowing roosters; cooing pigeons. Movies and books and the evening news prepared us for what a fucked-up city looked like. I was not ready for what it sounded like. Not the terror and the wailing and the crashing, that was expected. The silence. That awful absence of sound that announces your world has irreversibly changed. I heard it first just after Orion, then again sprawled out on the floor of my bedroom months, a year?, after burying Set.

It was the return of that grand silence that woke me out of my stupor. Everything else was still there: the macaws, the nighttime chorus of insects and amphibians, the rain and the skittering rodents. It was the adapted soundscape of Aguamictlan—the viejitos' low murmuring outside my door, their occasional singing along with the birds, their wrinkled but agile hands snipping leaves off the trees with rusted scissors and describing their uses—that I had again lost. They were gone.

I walked through the empty house and struggled to push open the front door against the overgrown bougainvillea. The sky was covered in platinum and silver rain clouds, casting a pale gray light over the neighborhood. Invasive chartreuse vines and dark spongy lichen climbed up the surrounding houses. Decomposed fruit covered the ground. In the back of the house, just opposite where I'd cocooned myself, the maracuya had started to climb the wall. One radiant purple sunburst bloomed from the vine. I knelt down to breathe the flower in, and stayed there for a while. Before rising, I kissed the flower and pinched un chingo de leaves off the vine.

I brewed the passionflower leaves with a near-fatal dose of jimson weed I'd found dangling over a fallen chain-link fence. Sitting still and alone on the rotting wooden steps where small white orchids bloomed from the bullet holes, I waited for the dead to come to me.

The first faint whisper came from the ground. *Sepaktli.*

I heard it again, louder with the backing track of the crickets and frogs. *Sepaktli.* I stood up and turned to the dense and dark forest in the east. *Find Sepaktli and wake your dead.* The light from the half-moon shone on a clear path to the abandoned Balam park. I stood up and followed the light.

Set's giant black-and-white-striped butterfly with red dots greeted me at the ticket booth. I ran my hands over its fro-

zen wings and lost the feeling in my legs. I fell forward into a
hill of militant red ants. *Keep moving, Maria*, they said as they
swarmed and pricked my hands. *You have to find her before she
finds you.* I shook them off and stumbled into the park, strug-
gling to keep my focus. I followed the flame-red ants as they
marched in the moonlight to a giant ceiba tree. I climbed over
its roots and, gripping the side of the thorny tree, I looked
down to a miniature moonlit beach buried deep in the earth.
The center of the park had caved in to reveal a cenote full of
fresh water. The clearing of thick trees allowed the moon to
shine directly in, revealing glints of little fish swimming in
the glowing blue. They caused the smallest ripples against
the muddy shore. Holding on to the tree's thick roots, I positioned myself at the edge of the sloping earth and slid down,
snagging the skinny vines of the invasive Golden Chalice
flowers on the way down. I landed on ground that was thick
and sticky as if the water had only recently receded. My eyes
adjusted to the underworld. The cave, and the water, stretched
deep and far beyond what I could see. Tiny turquoise bird
heads peeked out from the burrows within the amber cave
walls. When they realized I was not a threat, they emerged
from their homes and spread their wings to showcase their
brilliant plumage and catch the insects buzzing overhead.
Brown bats wrapped in their own winged cocoons hung sus-
pended from the ceiling, next to the stalactite tree roots. I
knelt down and cupped my hands in the water to drink. It
was cooler and sweeter than I could imagine, and the pool was
much deeper than I could see. I stared into the celestial pool
as if it were a scrying mirror. Soon the phantom white body

of a jellyfish emerged from the dark. I reached out my arm to greet our earliest ancestor and my fingers went through its body. How good it felt to be high. My mind didn't allow me to think of anything except color and light, my insides felt like velvet. I wrapped my arms around myself and closed my eyes. I realized too late that I was being watched. I turned my head as the golden crocodile languidly emerged, the water rolling off her metallic scales with faint plinks. I saw my reflection in her diamond eyes. "Señora de los Santos," I said, and bowed for no reason. "María."

Her sharp claws, her massive snout. Her body covered in shining scales and a rainbow of jewels. *Sepaktli!* She pulled her heavy body from the water and the ground shook. She positioned herself sideways on the treacly shore, blocking me from reaching the roots of the tree. The water lapped at the back of my ankles. I was trapped.

"Sepaktli," I corrected myself.

Jagged opalescent teeth lined her forever-smiling mouth. *You are suffering.* Her tail splashed against the water. *I give you this eternal pool, full of life.*

"Sepaktli," I pleaded. "I need you to bring back Set, the love of my life."

The crocodile lifted her head to gaze up at the ceiba tree. *And still, you want more.* The crocodile shuffled her feet and cracked her tail like a whip against my back. I fell forward into the sludgy muck and howled.

No life without sacrifice.

I tried to lift myself up on my hands and knees but failed, a current of pain shooting through my limbs. Sprawled out on my stomach, I reached for Sepaktli, her jaws inches from my face. She smelled me, her nostrils flaring, then retreated. *You're poisoned.* I watched her slink backward and recede into the dark water. *Bring me a child. Someone who shares your salty blood. Then I will revive your love from his earthly grave.* Her diamond eyes caught the moonlight as she disappeared.

I looked up at the short but improbable climb up the tree roots and began to drag myself toward the sloping earth. Behind me, the water sloshed. A small army of caimans emerged from the pool.

We don't usually get to choose our death. Approaching the end of four decades of life, I decided that I did not want to be eaten alive by a pack of crocodilians. I reached for the Golden Chalice flowers that hung like garlands from the ceiba's roots. I chewed on all the flowers I could fit into my mouth. The Golden Chalice works quick. Within moments I could no longer feel the pain in my back or the weight of my legs or the sharp teeth dragging me down to the water.

There is a phony supernova in our atmosphere, born from the noxious particles of the fiery rains and fumes released by the Orion quake. The optical illusion is locked in the sky above Aguamictlan and it changes hue with the time of day. Natalia says it is Oludumare's eye. I think it looks like a navel; we are trapped on the other side of the umbilical cord, waiting to be born.

The night of the caimans, I lost my connection to the dead and was reborn under that cosmic eye. A new body grew over my own. Celestial-blue fur dotted with black stars and rosettes.

Teeth that could tear through throats. Nose that could smell a creature's history through its sweat, eyes that could measure the content of a heart. It was always there, gestating and patiently waiting for my first death to finally be born.

When the Golden Chalice wore off, my new family knelt at my side. Natalia wrapped my shattered leg in coarse bark and a skinny black cat groomed fresh blood from his wounds. A trio of caimans roasted in a fire.

Aguamictlan's welcome sign looked like a tombstone framed by monstrous palm fronds. The earliest morning light washed over a lizard the size of a Chihuahua that lay stretched over the crumbling stone, its fat black-and-white-striped tail dangling over the *m*. A small pile of sun-bleached bird bones were heaped at the base of the sign. "Aguamictlan," Maite repeated to herself.

Aguamictlan.

Aguamictlan.

An incantation back into the world of green. The land of wild animals and buried moons from her childhood bedtime stories. The place where her mother roamed the streets telling fortunes for candy. The place, according to the heavy book in her bag, her aunt still called home. Maite inhaled the thick, hot smell of overripe fruit. The Mimilocas stretched their legs and made circles with their arms to fight back against any cramps from straining to cross the bridge. Their makeup and the sequins had fallen off during the trek, and Maite could match their voices to their faces. The opaque white of Burned Betty's left eye, the delicate cupid's bow of Nerieda's upper lip, Nacho's round cheeks dotted with a constellation of beauty marks. They could see her, too. See the ears she hadn't fully grown into, the heart-shaped face that would be like her mother's, the hollows under her cacao-seed eyes. "I've been here before," she said. "I came once with my mother."

"After Orion?" Nereida pulled her knee into her chest. "No one came here after the earthquake."

"Her sister lived here." Maite closed her eyes, desperate to remember any detail that might lead her closer to me, but still unwilling to share information about her mom. "Everything was green."

The Mimilocas finished stretching and continued on a pebbly road, past the moss-stained sides of abandoned buildings and gnarled trunks of ceiba trees. The temperature rose and Maite broke out into a sweat. Green parrots with hot-pink underwings flew overhead. "Escapees from the aviary at Balam," said Nacho. "It's abandoned now."

"By humans," clarified Burned Betty.

They walked toward a stone fountain full of rainwater and bathing sapphire birds. Next to it, a hand pump made from a bicycle handle and a fire hydrant. Nereida pumped the lever and Betty leaned down to take in handfuls of water, then splashed her face clean. When she finished, she pumped for Nereida. Nerieda for Nacho, Nacho for Maite. The water tasted sweeter than any water she'd ever drunk. "Where does your water come from?"

The Mimilocas simply pointed to the ground. Nacho continued to point out landmarks and shared snippets of local history that Maite was too overstimulated to retain. "That used to be the Plaza. Once a year, the viejitos used to host a big party and a parade to say goodbye to the old year and make room for the new. They don't do it anymore." He pointed to the cathedral. "That place had the best wood for bonfires."

"How do you know all this?"

"He's one of the viejitos' favorites," said Nereida.

"Nacho is everyone's favorite. He makes us look bad."

Nacho beamed. "All I do is ask one question, and *fwoosh!*

I get a whole history on things I'd never even thought of. Like Icelandic pop culture and how to hide our faces from computers."

"That's why you wear makeup?"

"We're getting in the habit. Don't know when Rio is going to start setting up surveillance again," said Nereida.

"And they will," said Burned Betty. "You saw those bill-boards, right? The desalination plant is next. The more Rio grows, the less of a chance we have to not get sucked up by them. They'll take everything."

They turned onto a palm-tree-lined street. Elaborate fences made of opaque plastic bottles and twisted car bumpers protected the bright-colored houses. The fiercer fences had broken bottles embedded into the tops of cement walls. One house had a rusted machine gun crowning the top of its gate. The Mimilocas waved to the hunched silhouettes of the viejitos emerging from their homes.

"Machete Maria protects you from Rio?"

Nacho hushed her. "Wait till we get to the Egg. The vieji-tos don't like when we talk about her."

"It's the *only* thing they don't talk about," mumbled Nereida. They continued down the wet road until the thick monsteras and spindly palms replaced the houses and the asphalt dissolved into a soppy dirt path. Maite's ankles felt weak. She struggled to get across the sloshy dirt. The Mim-ilocas were quiet, but Maite suspected they weren't as tired as she was, just unwilling to continue the conversation. The trees closed in on them, as if they were entering a part of Aguamict-lan not intended for humans. The Mimilocas seemed to be holding their breath for something, waiting for a signal that it was okay to speak again. Gray clouds rumbled overhead and released a fine drizzle. Maite stopped for a few moments of rest. She looked over the heads of the Mimilocas and saw it, the gleaming ivory egg in the middle of the forest.

The Egg's shell was streaked with bleached parrot droppings and dark brown mold. Invasive moss rose from its sunken base. The oxidized plaque on the front door confirmed Maite's suspicion:

Former home of the de los Santos family, founders of Rio de los Santos and first settlers of the Swamps of Sepaktli [present-day Aguamictlan].

Maite walked through the open wooden door. She pressed her palms against the Egg's interior. Cold and smooth. Thick wooden posts were embedded in the walls, stabilizing and grounding the Egg to the earth. She looked up and imagined the different rooms and levels according to the *Book of Marias*: the kitchen where Iara prepared food, the iron staircase a bejeweled Maria descended, the bathtub where she bathed next to Fernando's decapitated head. The round room was littered with dismantled computers, broken radios, steering wheels, an iron stove grate, an oven door, unrecognizable plastic, and other metal. In the center of the room was a raised wooden platform with bundles of blankets and tarps. "This is where you live?"

"It's our lab."

Thin beams of sunlight filtered in through the boarded-up windows. A faint scent of melted plastic and burnt meat lingered. Maite set her bag down on the platform and rummaged around. She pulled out a stick of palo santo and used her lighter to ignite it. A sweet smoke curled out from the stick. Burned Betty reached for the lighter, and Maite let her have it without protest. She put it in her pocket. "What do you know about Machete Maria?"

Maite considered pulling the book out of her duffel bag. She stopped herself and instead took out the shirt she'd stolen from Ciro's closet, and dabbed the back of her neck. She couldn't risk the Mimilocas taking the only connection she had to her family. "I think my mom told me the story when I was a kid. She killed her husband, right?"

Nereida knocked on one of the wooden posts. She read the etched sentences aloud: " 'Francisco de los Santos, great explorer of the Americas, traveled from Spain to the Amazon and the Orinoco River before setting his sights on the great new world of the north. His adventurous life met its gruesome end at the hands of his young Spanish wife, María de los Santos.' "

"So it's all true? She chopped off his head?"

"She chopped off his head *and* fed him to the crocodiles."

"Chopped off his head *and* her baby's head, then fed the crocodiles."

"She had a child?"

"No, that's why she lost her shit on poor Paco. I heard a version where she didn't die at all. Dragged down to the bottom of the swamps where the crocodiles made her a bog queen. She only comes up when she's hungry, and seduces men to eat them alive."

"Ew," said Maite.

"She's right," said Burned Betty, waving her finger in Maite's direction. "No one wants to fuck a bog bitch."

"But with a machete to your throat? You probably don't have a choice."

"The choice is machete," the Mimilocas said.

"What I don't understand," said Maite, raising her voice above the laughter, "is why aren't more people afraid of her? She still kills, doesn't she?"

Nacho kicked off his shoes and walked to the center of the platform. He sat cross-legged on top of a heap of blankets. "She hasn't killed us. She only hunts on the other side of the bridge. She's got a taste for rich meat."

"And why aren't the people in Rio afraid of her?"

Nereida shrugged. "I think they are afraid of her but not in the way you or I would be. I think they're deficient in fear. They don't have any salt in their blood." She undid the black ribbon holding up her ponytail. She tousled her fingers through her straight dark hair and stretched out next to Nacho. "They're hungry for that sweat, that rush of panic."

Nacho nodded in agreement. "One of the viejitas told me all about these rooms where people would pay all this money and have someone lock them in there while they figured out how to escape. They'd send in all sorts of scary shit, she said, like snakes and actors carrying knives. They can't enjoy their life unless they think it's about to be destroyed."

Maite sat down at the very edge of the platform. Her muscles twitched. "You're not afraid of Machete Maria?"

"Don't need to be. She's never hurt the viejitos. She's on our side," said Burned Betty.

Maite eyed a tower of gutted laptops and felt a jolt of danger hit her body. Nacho was right, it did feel good. "What exactly are you building?"

"We'll tell you what we're building if you tell us why you were trying to flee Rio."

Maite folded her legs up against her chest and wrapped her arms around her shins. "Not important," she said.

"Exactly," responded Betty.

Maite felt a soft thud against her back. She took the pillow Nereida had thrown at her and wrapped Clara's lavender blazer around it, then lowered her head and closed her eyes.

Maite followed Las Mimilocas through the dense and humid jungle. The sun was starting to set, and while she was relieved for the clean water and the chance to nap, she was annoyed at the Mimilocas for being annoyed at her. She pushed aside thin, pliable branches and shadowy leaves. Raindrops from the night before dripped from the towering banana trees onto Maite's head, and clumps of dirt clung to her silver sneakers. "You could've just told us from the start who you were."

"You shouldn't have gone through my stuff."

"There's no point to being so secretive. All our moms are dead."

"I had a feeling you were related," said Nacho. "I've only seen her once but you definitely look like her. Your eyes are the same."

Are. Are the same. Maite held back a smile. *My mother's sister is alive.*

"The viejitos say she's the reason we have clean water," said Burned Betty. "They said if it wasn't for her, we'd be skittering around Rio. Starving. Probably dead."

Maite waved away an aggressive white butterfly. The air felt thicker in this part of Aguamictlan. They'd walked into the forest beyond the Egg where, instead of bright homes with sharp fences, the vines and flowers had swallowed the abandoned casitas, turning them into blocks of house-shaped topiaries. "What happened to the people who lived here?"

"Almost everyone left after Orion and the fires. The viejitos who stayed behind eventually moved to the other side of the Egg," said Nacho. "They wanted to get away from all the creatures that escaped Balam. And now they take care of us."

Maite wiped off the sweat above her lip. "What kind of creatures?"

"Mostly cats. Jaguars, pumas, ocelots. Snakes and monkeys, too. Some of them were hunted. Most were captured. They keep them in cages at the Rio bank now. On display like living trophies," said Nereida.

Las Mimilocas passed the gates of an old and untended cemetery. Speckled fuchsia and bright white orchids bloomed on the mossy tombstones like hundreds of little spiders.

"But around here," Maite asked, "the cats are all gone?"

"All but one," said Nacho.

Betty stopped in her tracks and pointed to two Spanish-style casitas, the only ones that had a distinguishable shape and a visible front door. "Your aunt lives in one of those."

A sliver of a memory came into focus. Crayons and scraps of drafting paper. Maite thought, *I've been here before.* My silhouette appeared through the rusted screen door and I waited for my sister's daughter to bring me what I needed.

Maite and I sat in the center of my kitchen, where a carved and polished tree-trunk table grew from the ground. All the picture frames lining my walls contained comic strips that my grandfather had clipped to make himself laugh. Green vines with bright yellow flowers pierced through the cracked dirty window above the steel sink.

Maite held the leather-bound book. "Is this yours?"

"Your mom stole it from me."

"It's mostly blank pages."

"I know. Your mom stole it from me."

"Caracol is your husband's name?"

"No. It's mine." I drew a spiral in the air with my fingertip. "I am one Maria in a certain point in time. Then I am another. Your mother and I both told stories, just in different ways." I took my unfinished book from her hands. Her eyes lingered on my thick yellow nails. "Mine last longer."

"My mom is dead." Her dark brown eyes filled with tears. So much sadness in such a meaty little body.

I clicked my tongue and Lafcadio ran into the room and hopped on the table. He remained agile despite his heft. I scratched underneath his chin. His purr was a heavy bass and his meow like the ding of a triangle. "You can pet him," I said. I remembered how much I loved being around cats and dogs when I was Maite's age. MariLuz swore she was allergic, so we could never have furry animals in the house. I always befriended the strays.

Maite blinked back her tears and ran her hand over his black fur. "What do you call him?"

"Lafcadio. Sometimes I call him Laffy. Natalia, my neighbor, she named him Sombra. I think it's too simple a name for such an extraordinary cat. He doesn't seem to mind. He'll respond to anything."

"Kitty, kitty," sang Maite. She stroked behind his ears. "What happened to his eyes?" Maite pointed to the jagged scar accentuating his perpetually dilated right eye. The other eye looked reptilian. One full moon, one crescent.

"That's from the caimans. He saved my life fighting them off. Now he has an eye in both worlds."

"Like you? Were you like my mom?"

"I am nothing like MariLuz."

"You talk to the dead?"

I took a deep breath. "I could. At one time."

"Then how did you know my mom was dead? Did you talk to her?"

"She's my twin," I explained. But how would an only child understand what that meant? I was dragged into the water with her when the hurricane hit. I was there, in the lower left corner holding my breath, when my sister appeared to Maite in her lavender-walled bedroom thousands of miles away. I heard the final words Maria Lucia said to her daughter before their connection broke—*For you, for you.* I saw what my sister became.

"I just want to know why," said Maite. "Why did she leave the way she did?"

Careful careful. I couldn't scare her off, I couldn't make her cry. I couldn't scare myself off, either, couldn't leave an opening for this little girl to share what her dreams were made of or be endeared by the Y-shaped scar on her chin. For this task, *my* quest, I had succumbed to MariLuz's mantra to *play the game* and be *in it to win it*, fuck everyone else. I couldn't back down now. "Give me your hand."

I cupped Maite's palm in my own and traced the lines with my thumbs. "The dead are everywhere," I said. "I lost my connection to them years ago on the night of the caimans." I gently placed her hand on the wooden table and stood up to find something that used to roll around in the utensil drawer. I held up an opalescent orb the size of a tangerine. "This belonged to my abuelito Tomás." (It was part of a ten-dollar paperweight that broke years ago.) "He used it to speak to his ghosts. Including my grandmother." (Set bought the crystal ball paperweight for me as a joke when, after dating for a year, I admitted LaZuli was my sister.) "It allows you to see into another world." (Set said my stage name could be LaZirconia.) "Use it to see your mother. It is a way for her to find you and you to see her." I rolled the ball into Maite's open palm.

Maite held the orb into the light filtering in from the window. A ribbon of silver danced inside. Her mouth twitched into a half smile. "Thank you."

"It takes time to acclimate to the air here. Natalia will show you how to pull up water from the well and I'll set up a room for you."

"I've been here before."

"Yes," I said. "Your mom brought you here once."

Maite swatted at her arm. The mosquitoes were going to feast tonight. "So if my mom hadn't died, I wouldn't have seen you again?"

"Your mom didn't leave you so you could find me." I said this with a deliberate edge. I didn't want her thinking about fate and destiny. That kind of thinking produces the shrillest screams when you meet an unexpected end.

"What did my palm say?"

"Your palms are smooth," I said. "All I know for sure is they won't stay that way."

Maite's arms ached from pulling up the fresh water from the backyard well and carrying it into the porcelain bathtub. She heaped handfuls of Natalia's orange-peel-and-salt scrub on her body and sloughed off the sweat and mud she had accumulated since her last shower in the Acosta's granite and glass apartment. *Two days*, she thought. Only two days since she'd left the house she grew up in. How many hours of sleep? Not enough. She knocked out in the faded teal bedroom under a solar powered ceiling fan. When she woke up, the nocturnal insects serenaded her. Maite looked around the room, curious to see what the knickknacks and markings on the walls would reveal. She leaned in to inspect the origami flowers and creatures crowded on the wooden desk and admired their intricate rods and twists. *What patience*, thought Maite.

Let's make a paper crane. When I was Maite's age, I learned origami from one of the clerks at the Aguamictlan Public Library. She had strawberry-colored hair and an octopus tattooed on her chest, its arms curled around her throat. I think she was my grandfather's age. She kept a colorful collection of zines near the young adult section. All were lost in the fires.

Start with a square piece of paper.

This is a hamburger fold:

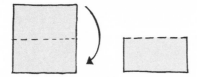

This is hot dog fold:

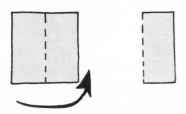

She said we could transform paper into anything.

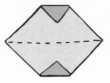

That it was an ancient technology. A witness and a transporter.

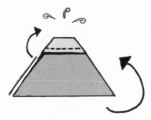

I've torn books apart to make my paper companions. I need something for my hands to do.

Idle hands . . .

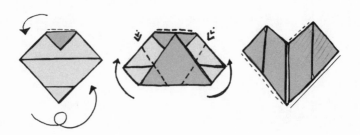

The men who killed Set lived in temporary canvas tents out-side the Egg. They'd been stationed there to survey the wreck-age of Orion and stitch Aguamictlan back together with the thin blue thread of irrelevant law.

I left a mess.

The viejitos said their murders must've been Machete Maria. They fell to their knees and babbled and prayed, speaking in tongues the investigating officers wouldn't try to understand. They called them *crazy religious superstitious stupid, let them die out in this shithole. We're done here.* The viejitos watched the remaining interstate officers pack up their tents and tanks and move on to Rio's ruins across the river.

Los viejitos me regañaron. If I wanted to remain in Agua-mictlan with them, they demanded I limit my hunting to capybaras. But what about the other side of the bridge? I asked. *Pues*—they shrugged their shoulders—*that's the other side of the bridge.*

When I start folding, I don't always know what it will be. Crease, fold, and unfold, pinch until something comes into focus.

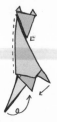

It can be whatever I want.

Whoever I want.

The paper takes on unexpected shapes. That's how it endures.

I am not afraid of who I've become.

If you tarot with the Pamela Colman Smith deck, the Wheel of Fortune card depicts a lion, an eagle, a snake, a ram, an angel, a sphinx, and the Egyptian god Anubis. The terrestrial, the amphibious, and the ecclesiastical cause the wheel to turn and the fates to align and divide. The simple truth of this card is that there is always movement. The Wheel of Fortune continuously spins and it doesn't spin on air and luck alone. It's weighted and pulled by the creatures surrounding you. In the Smith deck, the creatures are reading books. These are the same creatures that reappear in the World card. In other words, you can't fulfill the destiny promised in the Wheel of Fortune and arrive in a better World without stories and creatures.

The following morning, before the sun transformed the previous evening's rain to steam, Natalia and Maite sat together on the porch with a plate of freshly cut maracuya. Maite followed Natalia's lead and sucked the slimy pulp from the fruit.

"Maria lives two lives. When she eats the flowers, she becomes a beast."

"My mom was like that, too, after too much wine."

Natalia tucked her platinum hair behind her ear and smiled. "I bet she was."

I walked onto the porch, picking out bits of Golden Chalice from my teeth. "Do you really want to see your mother again?"

Taken aback, Maite only managed to nod. Natalia glared into the dark dilated pools of my eyes. She didn't know what the crocodile had promised me and I never explained. She was right to narrow her eyes at me, to be suspicious; I never took the Golden Chalice in the daytime. I ignored her. She confided in me once that she worried I would snap one day and start killing our neighbors. I was insulted. It was the only time we didn't speak for a whole day. But this was totally different. She wouldn't be able to sit so comfortably on that front patio if every time she looked up she, too, saw Set fall, break, bleed. A cruel memory loop, fallbreakbleed. If she did, she might not do what I was about to do to bring him back, but she wouldn't try to stop me.

Maite tightened her shoelaces and I bared my teeth to Natalia, daring her to intervene. Together, Maite and I walked toward the remains of Balam together. In one hand I held a dripping maracuya I'd swiped from Natalia, and in the other, my machete.

Rio, Aguamictlan, and the abandoned Balam are markers on the gradient scale of wilderness: Rio aspires to be an exotic fruit stand in an overpriced farmers' market. Aguamictlan is picking up ripened papaya from wet dirt, brushing off the bugs, and sinking your teeth in. Balam is a gargantuan monstera leaf concealing an emerald anaconda who hunts the rare red fruit of human hearts.

I hacked my way through the ropy green vines. I nudged Maite forward through the jaguar-mouth entrance of the old wildlife refuge. Shrouds of faded green moss and long spindly leaves dripped from the treetops like stage curtains to a botanist's fever dream. Towers of deep brown trunks rose like skyscrapers and a flurry of buzzing wings filled the air. Maite stood underneath a beam of light and lifted her face to the sky. She inhaled deeply. Crushed leaves and honeyed nectar. Decay. Rot. The faintest sound of running water.

For an instant I saw Maite not as my sister's daughter but as a small and singular creature, scared and alone in this world. A family of bright yellow parrots perched above the ticket booth began to squawk. I ran my hands over the red polka dots on the fiberglass butterfly wings. *Soon.* "This way," I said, and led us to the cenote.

Once we descended the roots of the ceiba tree and landed on the sludgy shore, I felt my body start to shift. A pale blue tint spread on my skin. The girl would not detect it. Her eyes weren't as sharp as mine. Maite knelt down and touched the water. She looked up at me for permission.

"Go ahead," I said. "It's fresh."

Maite cupped her hand to take a drink. "Where does it come from?"

"It has always been here." I set the machete down on the ground, close enough to reach, and drank from the pool.

"So this is where she lived," Maite said.

I tilted my head. "Who?"

"I read one of your stories. About María de los Santos." She gulped another handful of water. "Why do people think she's going around killing everyone?"

Sepaktli. The voice echoed in the cave. *What child calls my first name?* The water rippled and a gold shadow appeared just below the surface.

Maite rose slowly and I backed away from the water. She

clung to my arm. The water broke to reveal the massive snout of the golden crocodile, covered in shiny scales and a rainbow of jewels. The crocodile stepped toward us, its massive claws piercing the earth.

She opened her golden jaws:

I responded:

Maite looked up at me, her eyes wide and her bottom lip trembling. "Why am I here?"

"Sepaktli will reunite you with your mother."

Tears rolled down Maite's face. She clenched my arm even tighter. The crocodile watched us, smiling. I'd expected the girl to scream and wail, which would've made it easier to push her into the waters. Instead, she only let out quiet whimpers and petted the soft layer of fur emerging from my skin.

"Someone I love was taken from me," I said. "This is how I can bring him back."

Maite released her grip on my arm with such a force, I lost my footing. She backed away from me, one step closer to the crocodile. Her voice came out low and violent. "I'm not yours to give." The crocodile's tail swooshed in the water. The splash showered us, cool and clean. Maite picked up the machete by its handle and pointed it at the crocodile, who slinked back, her golden snout and diamond eyes floating above the water. Maite saw her own reflection in the blade. "Where did you get this?"

"Family heirloom," I said.

Maite looked closer at the machete's subtle serrations and blood rust. "It's you," she said. "You murdered those people in Rio."

"Murdered, relocated. Call it what you want."

She stabbed the air in my direction, warning me to step back. "You're Machete Maria."

The crocodile and I both smiled. "Right now, you are."

Maite looked at the blade in her hand and threw it to the ground.

Sepaktli snapped her jaws. *My child, come to me.* The crocodile pulled herself back up to the shore. *You won't suffer anymore.*

Maite wrapped her arms around herself and shook her head. "Nothing will change."

The crocodile's wide jaws creaked open.

"Nothing will change," Maite repeated.

I pictured a globe spinning on its axis. It spun without Set, would continue to spin without me. I saw the small light of the girl who understood what it could be. "I know why your mother died."

"She died because she was just like you. *Selfish.*" Maite knelt in front of the crocodile's open jaws and closed her eyes. "I don't want to end up hollow like you."

"Nature is unpredictable," I said. My eyes turned yellow and the fangs grew long and thick in my mouth. "That's why your mother died." My skin erupted in spotted blue fur and I lunged at the crocodile's neck. Maite clung to the ceiba tree roots and climbed up to the opening of the cenote, where she watched the blue jaguar and the golden crocodile battle until the sun rose.

THE FIRST MARIA

UNDER THE STARLIT SKY, the opalescent crocodile glided along the edges of the icy lagoon, guarding the Moon hidden below. Bejeweled with sapphires, amethyst, and beveled diamond eyes, the pearly-scaled behemoth amplified the Moon's pale light to illuminate the forest. Silver bats darted through the cool air of eternal night. Pearlescent blue snakes writhed and coiled across the mossy forest floor like rivers of ice. There was no fire or war; only life and darkness.

This is the time of Destruction.

Disguised as a comet, the Sun hunted the cosmos looking for the runaway Moon, determined to capture and control her. Passing over the land of darkness, he heard an enchanting song. The Sun shrunk himself into a small dot of light and saw the crocodile bathing in a waterfall, singing along to the notes of water hitting her ornate skin. He recognized the Moon's light refracted from the depths of the pool. His light expanded to the size of a tortoiseshell and sent rays to the crocodile's opaline body, surprising and delighting her. She sang louder. All the wild creatures arrived at the water's edge to listen to their beloved crocodile. The growing ball of light soared to the sky and swelled back into the boisterous Sun. *Bow before me!* The creatures fled to their burrows, their underwater lairs, the canopies of their trees. The lagoon water steamed and bubbled. *Bow before me, I am your king.*

The crocodile emerged from the warming water. Her skin dried instantly under the Sun's angry heat. *We belong to the dark.*

Bow before me, the Sun repeated. The tortoise, the cricket, the elephant, and the jaguar stood alongside the crocodile in the dried mud. *We have no king*, they responded in unison. The smooth skin of the elephant turned coarse and dry. The tortoise's sleek shell rippled and hardened. The jaguar's silver pelt crisped and broke out in dark boils, and the magnificent scales and jewels of the crocodile fell away; her bare skin rippled under the punishing Sun. *We have no king*, they repeated. They continued a silent defense of their land, soon joined by dozens of resolute birds and fish. Their resplendent feathers and bright scales dried and burned.

The Sun retreated to the cosmos, briefly returning the land to its darkness. The hidden creatures emerged from their burrows and lairs, and, upon seeing their transformed brothers and sisters, wept for their lost luminescence. Their tears transformed what remained of the freshwater lagoon into a salty sea. The Moon tasted the tears in her dreams and woke from her rest. She emerged from the water and rose over the forest. Seeing the scorched devastation caused by her tormentor, she wept. The tears splashed against the water and created eternally curling waves. *I will keep him away*, she promised. *One day, we will destroy him and return the land to darkness*. The creatures wailed as the Moon rose to the sky. She reflected the Sun's light back to him, blinding him and slowing him down in his endless pursuit of her. A gentle blue glow covered the land.

Wronged by the Sun and abandoned by the Moon, the creatures turned to each other for comfort and truth. But in this new light, all they saw were differences. How small some of them looked, how high-pitched their song, how erratic their movements. How delicate their skin, how succulent their meat. The creatures opened their jaws and tore into each other's flesh. They battled in the trees, chased each other in the burrows of the earth, and pushed each other into the water. The jaguar and crocodile paced and circled each other. They fought all night and the Moon mourned, powerless to pull them apart. Heartbroken, she retreated back into the cosmos. The Sun returned, satisfied with the war below.

Weak and weary from fighting each other, the creatures did not fight the Sun. They collapsed in his heat and slept in a near-death stupor all day. Once again, the Moon returned to blind the Sun, chasing him back to the cosmos. The jaguar and crocodile continued their battle under the moonlight, and, again, exhausted themselves. The Sun remained unchallenged. Each time the Moon arrived she turned her face away from the fighting and, at great risk to herself, dimmed her light to remind the creatures of their once-peaceful darkness. There were times when she didn't appear at all.

The crocodile and jaguar never heard the Moon's pleas above their grunts and howls. But the thousands of small silver fish who cleaned the surface of the Moon's brilliant face when she slumbered in their once-icy waters, they heard. With their pebble-sized mouths, the fish collected the dead skins and talons of the slaughtered creatures who fell limp and lifeless into the water from the land above. They assembled and stitched the patches of flesh into a creature unlike any in the forest, unlike any in the sea. The body of a serpent, the long-plumed tail of a bird, tortoiseshell scales, shiny black beetles as eyes, broken crocodile teeth, and splintered jaguar claws.

The fish waited for the Moon to show her full face and, using all their force, brought the monstrous offering of teeth and talons to the surface of the water. Her joyful tears crashed into the earth to make rivers and lagoons. Grateful to the loyal fish, the Moon cut her own face and gave a drop of blood to the creature. *Maria*, the Moon said. *My daughter. You will be my spirit in the water.* The creature twitched to life.

Cute.
I still think Machete Maria's story should be first.

When I was back in my fleshy body, Maite wrapped me in the remains of my clothes and helped me limp home. Natalia and Lafcadio greeted us with capybara skewers and jugo de mango. I ate and let Maite do the talking. It was her story as much as it was mine. I drank my passionflower tea and lay down to recover, lulled to sleep by the sound of their voices. I replayed my most treasured memory.

When we were newlyweds, Set and I drove across the country to New Orleans and did wonderful, terrible things to our bodies. I remember everything: dancing barefoot on Frenchmen Street, eating oysters after a day of drinking rainbow-colored drinks. Visiting haunted mansions and sleepy bayous. We cocooned ourselves in a fantasy world of music and ghosts and decadent foods. On our last day there, we visited the tomb of Marie Laveau. We were hungry, hungover, and without a guide. We fanned ourselves with tourist pamphlets and wandered around the City of the Dead until we found a huddled mass of people whispering around a five-foot-tall cement box. Etched slashes and X's drawn with chalk and lip liner decorated the eroded stone. Candies and candles, plastic beads, coins, and greasy little foil packets littered the base of the tomb. I grabbed Set's hand and pulled him closer. *This is it*, I remember saying. *I can feel it.* Because I could. There was a charge in the air.

"This is the tomb of Marie Le Faux," announced a passing tour guide. Slinking back, I followed along the tour and learned that the real resting place of the Voodoo Queen was a few yards away, marked by a simple and elegant plaque on a clean white marble tomb. A single silk red rose and three strands of purple and green beads lay at the base. I felt nothing in front of the real Marie's tomb. No cosmic force pulling my knees to the earth, no wavering light radiating from the grave. The myth surrounding that false grave saturated it with the weight and raw wants of its devotees. The tomb absorbed enough energy to create its own pull. I learned then what stories can do. They can create a separate reality. They can convince you to see only danger in a stranger's face or imbue power in coins and flimsy pieces of paper. They can guide us back to our animal selves.

How long will it take for someone to visit my sister's watery grave in Lake Pontchartrain and ask her to solve their problems? There might be airboats that go that way already, vulture tourists on a cruise to the sunken Crescent City. *Snorkel in the Creole Atlantis! See the brass band reef! Have your future read by the ghost of Marie Laveau! Dr. John! LaZuli!* She'd love that. I still don't want to hear shit from her. But her daughter does. The damp whispers in the cenote tell me that MariLuz will flex her bruja del mar status with a tidal wave during the next earthquake. Nature is unpredictable, but I know my sister. A tidal wave won't be enough.

MARIA DEL MAR

The first witch of the waters was born in Destruction. The moon named her Maria.

FOR MILLENNIA, Maria ruled over the primordial oceans and sewed together bits of the ancient animals to invent new beings: giraffes and platypuses, seahorses and zebras, cheetahs and men. The sea witch lives in the skeletal remains of a megalodon, her lair in the icy deep of the ocean, beyond the blind eels and stalactite-toothed angler fish and encircled by a river of toxic brine. Her throne is made of barnacled ship debris. At her side are maidens as old as your first ancestors, with a delicate pelt covering their bodies and canines jutting out from their bottom lips. They go where Maria sends them, riding on a phalanx of tireless mako sharks to shepherd the dead to their afterlife. Like the goddess Ma'at, Maria weighs the contents of drowned hearts to determine their fate. She reanimates the worthy ones and stitches together scales and fins to patch over the missing parts of their flesh. If the bodies are intact, she cracks off their human legs and tosses the limbs to the hungry barracudas. All are given fish tails. They begin a new life underwater as creatures of the sea. They live in peace. They don't remember their bodies but they do remember another world exists. They hunt, they speak, they make kingdoms.

One day, Maria found a bloated and grayed man in a coral garden. She sank her barracuda teeth into his chest and pulled out his heart. It was buoyant with promise and goodness. Maria changed her shape to a curvaceous fish woman and held the man in her arms while she stitched his chest back together. To patch over his heart, she used the iridescent scales of the queen angelfish. For his tail, she used the stately orca. The first, and only, King of the Sea. They lived in a coral-and-abalone palace, with a garden of anemones and urchins. She did not love him but knew she needed an heir. In her mermaid form, she gave birth to seven daughters. They were beautiful and kind. They could see futures and weave worlds from their dreams. But Maria could not imagine those simple creatures understanding the alchemy of the sea. The sea belonged to the cunning and bold. A creator and a destroyer. Disappointed that she failed to produce an appropriate successor, Maria left her inadequate daughters with their father in their coral-and-abalone palace without saying goodbye. She changed back to her original form and returned to her deep-sea lair, unconvinced she could continue her rule for another thousand years.

Weakened by her human father's ability to love, one of Maria's daughters grew up and fell for a human prince. Encouraged by a gossipy octopus and thrill-seeking oarfish, Marina braved the journey to the sea witch's lair to ask for a potion that would split her tail into two human legs. The sea witch recognized the face of her daughter, yet kept her true identity hidden. She asked Marina if she was willing to leave her family, her royalty, her beautiful anemone garden. *Would you break the hearts of those who love you to fulfill a selfish whim?*

Yes, Marina replied. *It is the only thing I can do.* The sea witch cackled and concocted a painful potion for her youngest daughter.

Three days of needles stabbing her enchanted legs. Three days of feeling the prince's fingers stroke her hair and graze her collarbone. One day for the prince to decide he would marry someone else.

On the prince's wedding night, Marina stood over the balcony and watched the dark waves swirl below. Her sisters appeared in the water, their skin reflecting the light of the full moon. A curling wave like an outstretched arm rose from the sea. It presented her with a bejeweled dagger. "Kill him, Marina. When his blood flows on your legs, you must return to the sea. Hurry."

Marina crept into the prince's bedroom and stood over his sleeping body, the outline of his new wife wrapped in a silk sheet. She crawled onto the bed and straddled him, clenching the bejeweled dagger in her hand. The stones cut into her palm. He looked like the marble carving she had in her garden. The garden she abandoned, the family she abandoned, the kingdom she left behind.

Marina raised the dagger over her head and plunged the knife into the sleeping prince's heart. His eyes opened wide and his mouth let out a choked sound, which Marina quickly smothered with her other hand. The prince did not suffer unnecessarily, just enough. When Marina pulled the knife from his chest, his blood gurgled from his body. Holding the blade in between her teeth, she removed her nightgown and cupped her hands over the fountain of his heart. She smeared his warm blood on her face, her breasts, the seams of her thighs. Marina felt her body stretch and shift to something new. She walked to the edge of the balcony and dove into the depths of the sea. The screams of the prince's fresh widow following her as she shattered the surface of the water.

The sea witch waited on her throne of sunken ships for Marina, the daughter that proved to be her true heir. She had prepared all that Marina needed to assume the role as la mera mera del mar: an inky potion that made her one with the sea, which Marina drank immediately; a deep cavern etched with all the names and souls of all the underwater creatures; and the promise to fulfill one of Marina's wishes. Marina spoke her wish. Maria laughed, reassured that she had chosen the rightful heir. She said, *Feed my blood to your sisters to make your wish come true.* Marina pierced the sea witch's heart with the bejeweled dagger. Blue and purple ribbons of blood slithered out of the bruja's chest, which Marina collected in a pale pink conch shell. She watched the sea witch transform back to the mysterious mother who had abandoned her family all those years before. She touched her mother's wild hair a final time before it drifted away, her luminous body rising to the surface of the sea, dissolving into the reflection of the moon.

Marina returned to her sisters to share that she had found their mother, that she was now at peace. The mermaids toasted to their mother's life and death. Marina passed around the conch shell and smiled as her sisters unknowingly drank their mother's blood. Within moments, their tails split into legs and their lungs filled with water. The swift makos seized the mermaids and sped them to shore. Naked and sputtering, the sisters cursed Marina. *Now we will rule on both land and sea*, Marina proclaimed. *You will share my secrets with your daughters and their daughters and on and on. From them, we will always have an heir, we will always rule the seas.*

When she was a child, the speck of seawater in Maria Lucia's veins told her that she was destined for an unimaginable greatness. She imagined herself a revered ruler of the seas and set out to rid herself of all that could interfere with her ascent, which was all that brought her joy: gummy bears, Barbie dolls, slumber parties, her sister.

To Maria Lucia, unexpected motherhood was like the tide. Some days, her love swelled and overwhelmed her. Other days, the tide pulled back and Maria Lucia stared at her daughter in silence, seeing only a helpless and heavy anchor. When the ocean demanded Maria Lucia sacrifice her daughter, she stood at the shore holding her newborn in her arms while the waves lapped hungrily against her feet. Maria Lucia agreed only to sacrificing life *with* her daughter, not her daughter's life. The sea accepted the exchange, and Maria Lucia lost her earthly life and the only person she loved.

As above, so below—Maria Lucia's rule is spectacular. She sends monsoons to claim islands and hurricanes to undo paper-thin edges of land. She stomps on tectonic plates and pokes at the earth's scabs. Lava flows. She is a tyrant and a drama queen—we are all at her mercy.

I wore the mask of a blue jaguar. Through the triangle-cut eyeholes, I watched my neighbors adjust their sparkling rainbow headdresses and tune their instruments. We all stood at the edge of Aguamictlan, the Rio Mictlan bridge stretching ahead of us. Some of the viejitos brought out their old instruments, the ones they played at the start of each new year. They brushed off sequins from the drumheads and loose feathers from the brass keys. The sun began its descent into the sea, washing us with orange and pink. We waited.

My sister always knew she would reign over the ocean after her first death, just like our grandfather knew he would reign over the skies. Just like María de los Santos chose the swamps and I chose the jungle. Daughters of Maria, we are never satisfied with one form. Maite wants the cities, and I agree that a pigeon is a noble choice. If she makes it through tonight, she will have a lifetime to decide.

One of the viejitas let out a shout and waved to the other side of the bridge. We watched the distant elastic shadows of the Mimilocas bend and leap over the serrated concrete. Maite's silver duffel bag reflected the fading daylight and my jaw unclenched at the sight of her. They were moving faster than usual, racing back to Aguamictlan after setting their bombs. Natalia and I stood alongside the viejitos, holding our breath until they returned.

The Mimilocas had reached the middle of the bridge when we heard the first boom. The viejitos dropped their instruments and held out their hands to steady each other. *Boom,*

boom, came the second and third explosions. We recoiled, but we were safe. The Mimilocas popped back into view and we heard them cheer. The viejitos pointed to the plumes of smoke rising into the sky and began to clap. The Mimilocas continued toward us, darting and laughing over the mangled steel. That's when I saw them. The big cats of Balam. They appeared at the edge of Rio, emaciated and disoriented. The familiar scent of blooming orchids and wild capybara called to them. I took off my mask and watched them, my wild kin, pacing at the riverbed's sticky sludge, unsure of what waited for them on the other side. I paced with them.

The sun had set and turned the sky lavender. I heard the Mimilocas' heavy breathing as they pulled themselves up from the muddy edge of Aguamictlan. I took a deep breath and stepped forward, away from Natalia and the viejitos, and let out a low and rumbling growl. The big cats paused and raised their heads. Silence. The viejitos pulled on their masks: tigers and orangutans, lemurs and sharks, children and friends—the faces of our extinct beings. The earth jolted and shook at our feet. We steadied ourselves and called to the lost creatures of Balam. A trumpet blared and a snare drum rattled. The viejitos knelt and played their instruments on the ground, slow and deep, mimicking the vibrations of the jungle. *Come home, Come home.* I heard a distant guttural rumble and I growled again in response. *Come home.* The jaguars leapt toward Aguamictlan. We clapped our hands and stomped our feet, then turned to run. In a dizzying blur of colorful feathers and clanging instruments, we raced back to our homes and climbed atop the roofs and the high branches of the ceiba trees.

We caught glimpses of the spotted pelts of the jaguars and the velvety black of the pumas. The yelps of the tamarins and the hiss of the anacondas. Sepaktli would no longer be alone in guarding her hidden waters. The earth shook again, one violent lurch forward. Our homes and trees only trembled. We were far enough away to be spared Mari-Luz's flamboyant debut. Her tsunami ripped through Rio, dragging all that remained back to her deep-sea lair.

We saw the flashes of Rio's neon lights pop and fade. Darkness. Below us, rustling leaves and the final cry of capybaras. Alguien echó un grito and the viejitos returned the shout. We exploded into a rowdy tamborazo and welcomed back the night.

* * *

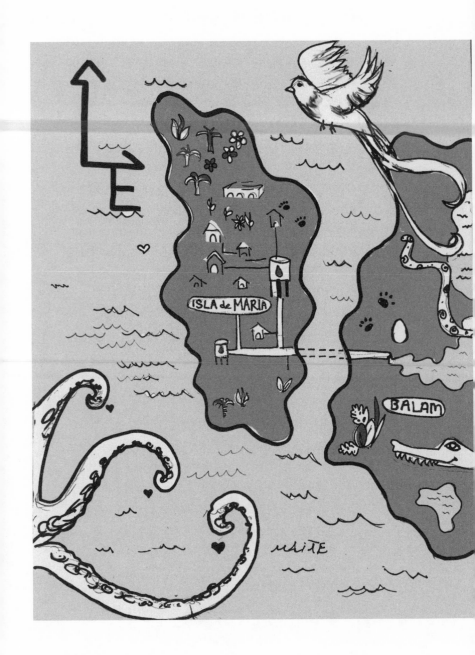

Acknowledgments

Monica Odom, I thank you for believing in my stories and for being the first "yes" that made this book possible. Thank you, Gina Iaquinta, for your incredible intuition and wicked sense of humor. Thank you, Monica, Gina, and the Liveright team for your compassionate support in helping me complete this book in a challenging and unexpected moment in time.

Abrazos to my patient coworkers who picked up the slack when I took time off to write: Caroline Kim, Kathy Honda, Nicole Connolly, Christina Catabay, Emily Neely, and Chloe Saalsaa. Gratitude across space and time for the bosses who respected my creativity: Bea Calderon, John Kim, Jason Holland, and Casey Reitz.

Black cat purrs to my otherworldly friends who always came through with a new tarot deck or Surrealist artwork: Angela Mary Magick, Dan and Ashlee Weisz, Annabella Pritchard. Chilo and Adriana, thank you for always being so kind to me and Greg, and for all the thought-provoking art you both consistently create. Julie Leopo, thank you for always having my back.

Davin Malasarn and Libby Flores, I love you both and will always be grateful to PEN America for bringing us together. Thank you to Michelle Franke, Hilary Holley, Heather Simons, Sasha Mann. Shanna, we all still love you.

Carlos and Luke, I can't imagine my life without you two! I can finally say I have college friends. And because of the Queens MFA program in South America, I can finally say I went to college. Thank you to Ada Limón, Héctor Tobar, Francisco Goldman, Manuel Gonzalez, Mary Gaitskill, Maxine Swann, Fred Leebron, and Gisele Firmino.

The following institutions were good to me, being good to them helps support other writers: PEN America, Bread Loaf Writers' Conference and the Rona Jaffe Foundation, *Kweli Journal*, and VONA.

All the flowers for my beautiful mother, who is a sharp and relentless critic and never lets me take the easy route. Para mi papá, gracias por todas las pláticas y los wafflers. Gracias a Mama Cuca and Grandma Lucy for your wisdom. Thank you to Melissa for never letting my head get too big that it suffocates my imagination.

Thanks to my truest friend and love of my life, Greg Camphire. Extraordinary and full of light. I will ask you, reader, to draw at least one of the following in an empty page of this book:

- *A lemur with a heart-shaped tail*
- *A crocodile holding birthday balloons*
- *A pinniped of your choosing*

And now you also know what it feels like to create joy where there was only blank space before.